Explorers of the Dawn

Mazo De la Roche

Explorers of the Dawn

ISBN: 978-1-64799-698-7

CONTENTS

Chap.		
	Foreword	iv
I	Buried Treasure	1
II	The Jilt	24
III	Explorers of the Dawn	39
IV	A Merry Interlude	53
V	Freedom	70
VI	D'ye Ken John Peel	90
VII	Granfa	107
VIII	Noblesse Oblige	127
IX	The Cobbler and His Wife	147
X	The New Day	163

Foreword

The publisher has asked me to write a note of introduction to this book. Surely it needs none; but it is a pleasant task to write prefaces for other people's books. When one writes a preface to a book of one's own, one naturally grovels, deprecates, and has no opportunity to call the friendly reader's attention to what the author considers the beauties and significances of the work. How agreeable, then, to be able to do this service for another.

Moreover, one hopes that such a service may not be wholly vain. Every book has its own special audience, for whom—very likely unconsciously—it was written: the group of people, far spread over the curve of earth, who will find in that particular book just the sort of magic and wisdom that they seek. And, as every one who has studied the book business knows, books very often tragically miss just the public that was waiting for them. It is such an obscure and nebulous problem, getting the book into the hands of the people to whom it will appeal. One knows that there are thousands of readers for whom that book (whatever it may be) will mean keen pleasure. But how is one to find them and bring the volume to their eyes?

I owe to the "Atlantic Monthly" my own introduction to Miss de la Roche's writing. Several years ago, when I was acting as a modest periscope for a publishing house, I read in the "Atlantic" a fanciful little story by her which seemed to me so delicate and humorous in fancy, so refreshing and happy in expression, that I wrote to the author in the hope of some day luring her to offer a book to the house with which I was connected. We had some pleasant correspondence. Time passed: I fell from the placid ramparts of the publishing business, into the more noisy but not less happy bustle of the newspaper world. But still, though I am not a conscientious correspondent, I managed to keep occasionally in touch with Miss de la Roche. For a while I seemed highly unsuccessful as her ambassador into the high court of publishing. Then, one day, lunching with Mr. Alfred Knopf at a small tavern on Vesey Street (which was subsequently abolished by the New York City Health Department as being unfit to offer what one of the small boys in this book calls "nushment") I happened to tell him about Miss de la Roche's work. I saw his eye, an eye of special clarity and brilliance, widen and darken with that particular emotion exhibited by a publisher who feels what is vulgarly known as a "hunch." He said he would "look into" the matter; and this book is the result.

The phrase "look into" is perhaps appropriate as applied to this book. For it is one of those books where the eye of the attentive reader sees more than a mere sparkling flow of words on a running surface of narrative. Of course this is not one of those books that "everybody must read." It is not likely to become fashionable. But it seems to me so truly charming, so felicitous in subtle touches of humour, so tenderly moved with an under-running current of wistfulness, that surely it will find its own lovers; who will be, perhaps, among those who utter the names of Barrie and Kenneth Grahame with a special sound of voice.

Perhaps, since I myself was one of a family of three boys, the story of Angel, Seraph and John, makes a prejudicial claim upon my affection. I must admit that it is evident the author of the book was never herself a small boy: sometimes their imperfections are a little too perfect, too femininely and romantically conceived, to make me feel one of them. They have not quite the rowdy actuality of Mr. Tarkington's urchins. But the, fact that the whole story is told with a poet's imagination, and viewed through a golden cloud of fancy, gives us countervailing beauties that a strictly naturalistic treatment would miss. Let us not forget that we are in a "Cathedral Town"; and next door is a Bishop. And certainly in the vigorous and great-hearted Mary Ellen we stand solidly on the good earth of human nature "as is."

It is not the intention of the introducer to anticipate the reader's pleasure by selfishly pointing out some of the dainty touches of humour that will arouse the secret applause of the mind. One thing only occurs to be said. The scene of the tale is said to be in England. And yet, to the zealous observer, there will seem to be some flavours that are hardly English. The language of the excellent Mary Ellen, for instance, comes to me with a distinct cisatlantic sound. Nor can I, somehow, visualize a planked back garden in an English Cathedral Town. I am wondering about this, and I conclude that perhaps it is due to the fact that Miss de la Roche lives in Toronto, that delightful city where the virtues of both England and America are said to be subtly and consummately blended. Her story, as simple and refreshing as the tune of an old song, and yet so richly spiced with humour, perhaps presents a blend of qualities and imaginations that we would only find in Canada; for the Canadians, after all, are the true Anglo-Americans. Perhaps they do not like to be called so? But I mean it well: I mean that they combine the good qualities of both sides.

And so one wishes good fortune to this book in its task—which every book must face for itself—of discovering its destined friends. There will be some readers, I think, who will look through it as through an open window, into a land of clear gusty winds and March sunshine and volleying church bells on Sunday mornings, into a land of terrible contradictions, a land whose emigrés look back to it tenderly, yet without too poignant regret—the Almost Forgotten Land of childhood.

Christopher Morley

Chapter I

Buried Treasure

I

Probably our father would never have chosen Mrs. Handsomebody to be our governess and guardian during the almost two years he spent in South America, had it not seemed the natural thing to hand us over to the admirable woman who had been his own teacher in early boyhood.

Had he not been bewildered by the sudden death of our young mother, he might have recalled scenes between himself and Mrs. Handsomebody that would have made him hesitate to leave three stirring boys under her entire control. Possibly he forgot that he had had his parents, and a doting aunt or two, to pad the angularities of Mrs. Handsomebody's rule, and to say whether or not her limber cane should seek his plumpest and most tender parts.

Then, too, at that period, Mrs. Handsomebody was still unmarried. As Miss Wigmore she had not yet captured and quelled the manly spirit of Mr. Handsomebody. From being a blustering sort of man, he had become, Mary Ellen said, very mild and fearful.

On his demise Mrs. Handsomebody was left in solitary possession of a tall, narrow house, in the shadow of the grey Cathedral in the rather grey and grim old town of Misthorpe. Here, Angel and The Seraph and I were set down one April morning, fresh from the country house, where we had been born; our mother's kisses still warm, one might say, on our round young cheeks.

Unaccustomed to restraint, we were introduced into an atmosphere of drabness and restraint, best typified, perhaps, by the change from our tender, springy country turf, to the dry, blistered planks of Mrs. Handsomebody's back yard. Angel, fiery, candid, inconstant; the careless possessor of a beautiful boys' treble, which was to develop into the incomparable tenor of today—next, myself, a year younger, but equally tall and courageous, in a more dogged way—then, The Seraph, three years my junior, he was just five, following where we led with a blind loyalty, "Stubborn, strong and jolly as a pie."

1

Truly when I think of us, as we were then, and when I remember how we came like a wild disturbing wind into that solemn house, I am inclined to pity Mrs. Handsomebody.

Even when she sent us to bed in the colossal four-poster, in the middle of the afternoon, we were scarcely downcast, for it was not such a bad playground after all, and by drawing the curtains, we could shut ourselves completely away from the world dominated by petticoats.

Then there was Mary Ellen, with her "followers," always our firm ally, brimming with boisterous good health. Looking back, I am convinced that Mrs. Handsomebody deserves our sympathy.

II

It was Saturday morning, and we three were in Mrs. Handsomebody's parlour—Angel, and The Seraph, and I.

No sooner had the front door closed upon the tall angular figure of the lady, bearing her market basket, than we shut our books with a snap, ran on tiptoe to the top of the stairs, and, after a moment's breathless listening, cast our young forms on the smooth walnut bannister, and glided gloriously to the bottom.

Regularly on a Saturday morning she went to market, and with equal regularity we cast off the yoke of her restraint, slid down the bannisters, and entered the forbidden precincts of the Parlour.

On other week days the shutters of this grim apartment were kept closed, and an inquisitive eye, applied to the keyhole, could just faintly discern the portrait in crayon of the late Mr. Handsomebody, presiding, like some whiskered ghost, over the revels of the stuffed birds in the glass case below him.

But on a Saturday morning Mary Ellen swept and dusted there. The shutters were thrown open, and the thin-legged piano and the haircloth furniture were furbished up for the morrow. Moreover Mary Ellen liked our company. She had a spooky feeling about the parlour. Mr. Handsomebody gave her the creeps, she said, and once when she had turned her back she had heard one of the stuffed birds twitter. It was a gruesome thought.

When we bounded in on her, Mary Ellen was dragging the broom feebly across the gigantic green and red lilies of the carpet, her bare red arms moving like listless antennæ. She could, when she willed, work vigorously and well, but no one knew when a heavy mood might seize her, and render her as useless as was compatible with retaining her situation.

"Och, byes!" she groaned, leaning on her broom. "This Spring weather do be makin' me as wake as a blind kitten! Sure, I feel this mornin' like as if I'd a stone settin' on my stomach, an' me head feels as light as thistledown. I wisht the missus'd fergit to come home an' I could take a day off—but there's no such luck for Mary Ellen!"

She made a few more passes with her broom and then sighed.

"I think I'll soon be lavin' this place," she said.

A vision of the house without the cheering presence of Mary Ellen rose blackly before us. We crowded round her.

"Now, see here," said Angel masterfully, putting his arms about her stout waist. "You know perfectly well that father's coming back from South America soon to make a home for us, and that you are to come and be our cook, and make apple-dumplings, and have all the followers you like."

Now Angel knew whereof he spoke, for Mary Ellen's "followers" were a bone of contention between her and her mistress.

"Aw, Master Angel," she expostulated, "What a tongue ye have in yer head to be sure! Followers, is it? Sure, they're the bane o' me life! Now git out av the way o' the dust, all of yez, or I'll put a tin ear on ye!" And she began to swing her broom vigorously.

We ran to the window and looked out but no sooner had we looked out than we whistled with astonishment at what we saw.

First you must know that on the west of Mrs. Handsomebody's house stood the broad, ivy-clad mansion of the Bishop, grey stone, like the Cathedral; on the east was a dingy white brick house, exactly like Mrs. Handsomebody's. In it lived Mr. and Mrs. Mortimer Pegg and their three servants.

To us they seemed very elegant, if somewhat uninteresting people. Mrs. Mortimer Pegg frequently had carriage callers, and not seldom

3

sallied forth herself in a sedate victoria from the livery stables. But beyond an occasional flutter of excitement when their horses stopped at our very gate, there was little in this prim couple to interest us. So neat and precise were they as they tripped down the street together, that we called them (out of Mrs. Handsomebody's hearing) Mr. and Mrs. "Cribbage" Pegg.

Now, on this morning in mid-spring when we looked out of the window our eyes discovered an object of such compelling interest in the Pegg's front garden that we rubbed them again to make sure that we were broad awake.

Striding up and down the small enclosure was a tall old man wearing a brilliant-hued, flowered dressing-gown, that hung open at the neck, disclosing his long brown throat and hairy chest, and flapping negligently about his heels as he strode.

He had bushy iron-grey hair and moustache, and tufts of curly grey beard grew around his chin and ears. His nose was large and sun-burned; and every now and again he would stop in his caged-animal walk and sniff the air as though he enjoyed it.

I liked the old gentleman from the start.

"Oo-o! See the funny old man!" giggled The Seraph. "Coat like Jacob an' his bwethern!"

Angel and I plied Mary Ellen with questions. Who was he? Did he live with the Peggs? Did she think he was a foreigner? Mary Ellen, supported by her broom, stared out of the window.

"For th' love of Hiven!" she ejaculated. "If that ain't a sight now! Byes, it's Mr. Pegg's own father come home from somewheres in th' Indies. Their cook was tellin' me of the time they have wid him. He's a bit light-headed, y'see, an' has all his meals in his own room—th' quarest dishes iver—an' a starlin' for a pet, mind ye."

At that moment the old gentleman perceived that he was watched, and saluting Mary Ellen gallantly, he called out:

"Good-morning, madam!"

Mary Ellen, covered with confusion, drew back behind the curtain. I was about to make a suitable reply when I saw Mrs. Mortimer Pegg, herself, emerge from her house with a very red face, and resolutely grasp her father-in-law's arm. She spoke to him in a rapid

4

undertone, and, after a moment's hesitation, he followed her meekly into the house.

How I sympathized with him! I knew only too well the humiliation experienced by the helpless male when over-bearing woman drags him ignominiously from his harmless recreation.

A bond of understanding seemed to be established between us at once.

The voice of Mary Ellen broke in on my reverie. She was teasing Angel to sing.

"Aw give us a chune, Master Angel before th' missus gets back! There's a duck. I'll give ye a pocket full of raisins as sure's fate!"

Angel, full of music as a bird, could strum some sort of accompaniment to any song on the piano. It was Mary Ellen's delight on a Saturday morning to pour forth her pent up feelings in one of the popular songs, with Angel to keep her on the tune and thump a chord or two.

It was a risky business. But The Seraph mounted guard at the window while I pressed my nose against the glass case that held the stuffed birds and wondered if any of them had come from South America. "How jolly," I thought, "to be there with father."

Tum-te-tum-te-tum, strummed Angel.

> *"Casey would waltz with the strawberry blonde,*
> *And the—band—played—on."*

His sweet reedy tones thrilled the April air.

And Mary Ellen's voice, robust as the whistle of a locomotive, bursting with health and spirits, shook the very cobwebs that she had not swept down.

> *"Casey would waltz with th' strawberry blonde,*
> *And—the—band—play—don!"*

Generally we had a faithful subordinate in The Seraph. He had a rather sturdy sense of honour. On this spring morning however, I think that the singing of Mary Ellen must have dulled his sensibilities, for, instead of keeping a bright lookout up the street for the dreaded form of Mrs. Handsomebody, he lolled across the

5

window-sill, dangling a piece of string, with the April sunshine warming his rounded back.

And as he dangled the string, Mrs. Handsomebody drew nearer and nearer. She entered the gate—she entered the house—she was in the parlour!!

Angel and Mary Ellen had just given their last triumphant shout, when Mrs. Handsomebody said in a voice of cold fury:

"Mary Ellen, kindly cease that ribald screaming. David (David is Angel's proper name) get up instantly from that piano stool and face me! John, Alexander, face me!"

We did so tremblingly.

"Now," said Mrs. Handsomebody, "you three boys go up to your bedroom—not to the schoolroom, mind—and don't let me hear another sound from you today! You shall get no dinner. At four I will come and discuss your disgraceful conduct with you. Now march!"

She held the door open for us while we filed sheepishly under her arm. Then the door closed behind us with a decisive bang, and poor Mary Ellen was left in the torture-chamber with Mrs. Handsomebody and the stuffed birds.

III

Angel and I scurried up the stairway. We could hear The Seraph panting as he laboured after us.

Once in the haven of our little room we rolled in a confused heap on the bed, scuffling indiscriminately. It was a favourite punishment with Mrs. Handsomebody, and we had a suspicion that she relished the fact that so much food was saved when we went dinnerless. At any rate, we were not allowed to make up the deficiency at tea-time.

We always passed the hours of our confinement on the bed, for the room was very small and the one window stared blankly at the window of an unused room in the Peggs' house, which blankly returned the stare.

6

But these were not dull times for us. As Elizabethan actors, striding about their bare stage, conjured up brave pictures of gilded halls or leafy forest glades, so we little fellows made a castle stronghold of our bed; or better still, a gallant frigate that sailed beyond the barren walls into unknown seas of adventure, and anchored at last off some rocky island where treasure lay hid among the hills.

What brave fights with pirates there were, when Angel as Captain, I as mate, with The Seraph for a cabin boy, fought the bloody pirate gangs on those surf-washed shores, and gained the fight, though far out-numbered!

They were not dull times in that small back room, but gay-coloured lawless times, when our fancy was let free, and we fought on empty stomachs, and felt only the wind in our faces, and heard the creak of straining cordage. What if we were on half-rations!

On this particular morning, however, there was something to be disposed of before we got to business. To wit, the rank insubordination of The Seraph. It was not to be dealt with too lightly. Angel sat up with a dishevelled head.

"Get up!" he commanded The Seraph, who obeyed wonderingly.

"Now, my man," continued Angel, with the scowl that had made him dreaded the South Seas over, "have you anything to say for yourself?"

The Seraph hung his head.

"I was on'y danglin' a bit o' stwing," he murmured.

"String"—repeated Angel, the scowl deepening, "dangling a bit of string! You may be dangling yourself at the end of a rope before the sun sets, my hearty! Here we are without any dinner, all along of you. Now see here, you'll go right over into that corner by the window with your face to the wall and stand there all the time John and I play! An'—an' you won't know what we're doing nor where we're going nor anything—so there!"

The Seraph went, weeping bitterly. He hid his face in the dusty lace window curtain. He looked very small. I could not help remembering how father had said we were to take care of him and not make him cry.

Somehow that morning things went ill with the adventure. The

7

savour had gone out of our play. Two were but a paltry company after all. Where was the cabin-boy with his trusty dirk, eager to bleed for the cause? Though we kept our backs rigorously turned to the window, and spoke only in whispers, neither of us could quite forget the presence of that dejected little figure in the faded holland smock.

After a bit The Seraph's whimpering ceased, and what was our surprise to hear the chuckling laugh with which he was wont to signify his pleasure!

We turned to look at him. His face was pressed to the window, and again he giggled rapturously.

"What's up, kid?" we demanded.

"Ole Joseph-an'-his-Bwethern," he sputtered, "winkin' an' wavin' hands wiv me!"

We were at his side like a shot, and there in the hitherto blank window of the Peggs' house stood the old gentleman of the flowered dressing-gown laughing and nodding at The Seraph! When he saw us he made a sign to us to open our window, and at the same instant raised his own.

It took the three of us to accomplish it, for the window moved unreadily, being seldom raised, as Mrs. Handsomebody regarded fresh air much as she regarded a small boy, as something to be kept in its place.

At last the window rose, protesting and creaking, and the next moment we were face to face with our new acquaintance.

"Hello!" he said, in a loud jovial voice.

"Hello!" said we, and stared.

He had a strong, weather-beaten face, and wide-open light eyes, blue and wild as the sea.

"Hello, boy!" he repeated, looking at Angel, "What's your name?"

Now Angel was shy with strangers, so I usually answered questions.

"His name," I replied then, "is David Curzon but mother called him Angel, so we jus' keep on doing it."

8

"Oh," said the old gentleman. Then he fixed The Seraph with his eye. "What's the bantling's name?"

The Seraph, mightily confused at being called a bantling, giggled inanely, so I replied again.

"His name is Alexander Curzon, but mother called him The Seraph, so we jus' keep on doing it too."

"Um-hm," assented the old gentleman, "and you—what's your name?"

"John," I replied.

"Oh," he said, with an odd little smile, "and what do they keep on calling you?"

"Just John," I answered firmly, "nothing else."

"Who's your father?" came the next question.

"He's David Curzon, senior," I said proudly, "and he's in South America building a railroad an' Mrs. Handsomebody used to be his governess when he was a little boy, so he left us with her, but some day, pretty soon, I think, he's coming back to make a really home for us with rabbits an' puppies an' pigeons an' things."

Our new friend nodded sympathetically. Then, quite suddenly, he asked:

"Where's your mother?"

"She's in Heaven," I answered sadly, "she went there two months ago."

"Yes," broke in The Seraph eagerly, "but she's comin' back some day to make a weally home for us!"

"Shut up!" said Angel gruffly, poking him with his elbow.

"The Seraph's very little," I explained apologetically, "he doesn't understand."

The old gentleman put his hand in the pocket of his dressing-gown.

"Bantling," he said with his droll smile, "do you like peppermint bull's-eyes?"

9

"Yes," said The Seraph, "I yike them—one for each of us."

Whereupon this extraordinary man began throwing us peppermints as fast as we could catch them. It was surprising how we began to feel at home with him, as though we had known him for years.

He had travelled all over the world it seemed, and he brought many curious things to the window to show us. One of these was a starling whose wicker cage he placed on the sill where the sunlight fell.

He had got it, he said, from one of the crew of a trading vessel off the coast of Java. The sailor had brought it all the way from Devon for company, and, he added—"the brute had put out both its eyes so that it would learn to talk more readily, so now, you see, the poor little fellow is quite blind."

"Blind—blind—blind!" echoed the starling briskly, "blind—blind—blind!"

He took it from its cage on his finger. It hopped up his arm till it reached his cheek, where it began to peck at his whiskers, crying all the while in its shrill, lonely tones,—"Blind, blind, blind!"

We three were entranced; and an idea that was swiftly forming in my mind struggled for expression.

If this wonderful old man had, as he said, sailed the seas from Land's End to Ceylon, was it not possible that he had seen, even fought with, real pirates? Might he not have followed hot on the trail of hidden treasure? My cheeks burned as I tried to put the question.

"Did you—" I began, "did you—"

"Well?" he encouraged. "Did I what, John?"

"Oh, did you," I burst out, "ever see a pirate ship, an' pirates—real ones?"

His face lit up.

"Surely," he replied casually, "many an one."

"P'raps—" ventured Angel, with an excited laugh, "p'raps you're one yourself!"

The old gentleman searched our eager faces with his wide-open, sea

10

blue eyes, then he looked cautiously into the room behind him, and, apparently satisfied that no one could overhear, he put his hand to the side of his mouth, and said in a loud hoarse whisper—

"That I am. Pirate as ever was!"

I think you could have knocked me down with a feather. I know my knees shook and the room reeled. The Seraph was the first to recover, piping cheerfully—

"I yike piwates!"

"Yes," repeated the old gentleman, reflectively, "pirate as ever was. The things I've seen and done would fill the biggest book you ever saw, and it'd make your hair stand on end to read it—what with fights, and murders, and hangings, and storms, and shipwreck, and the hunt for gold! Many a sweet schooner or frigate I've sunk, or taken for myself; and there isn't a port on the South Seas where women don't hush their children crying with the fear of Captain Pegg."

Then he added hastily, as though he feared he had gone too far:

"But I'm a changed man, mark you—a reformed man. If things suit me pretty well here I don't think I shall break out again. It is just that you chaps seem so sympathetic makes me tell you all this; but you must swear never to breathe a word of it, for no one knows but you. My son and daughter-in-law think I'm an archæologist. It'd be an awful shock to them to find that I'm a pirate."

We swore the blackest secrecy, and were about to ply him with a hundred questions, when we saw a maid carrying a large tray enter the room behind him.

Captain Pegg, as I must now call him, gave us a gesture of warning and began to lower his window. A pleasant aroma of roast beef came across the alley. The next instant the flowered dressing-gown had disappeared and the window opposite stared blankly as before.

Angel blew a deep breath. "Did you notice," he said, "how different he got once he had told us he was a pirate—wilder and rougher, and used more sailor words?"

"However did you guess it first?" I asked admiringly.

11

"I think I know a pirate when I see one," he returned loftily. "But, oh I say, wouldn't Mrs. Handsomebody be waxy if she knew?"

"An' wouldn't Mary Ellen be scared stiff if she knew?"

"An' won't we have fun? Hurray!"

We rolled in ecstasy on the much-enduring bed.

We talked excitedly of the possibilities of such a wonderful and dangerous friendship. And as it turned out, none of our imaginings equalled what really happened.

The afternoon passed quickly. As the hands of our alarm clock neared the hour of four we obliterated the traces of our sojourn on the bed as well as we could, and, when Mrs. Handsomebody entered, she found us sitting in a row on the three cane-bottomed chairs, on which we hung our clothes at night.

The scolding she gave us was even longer and more humiliating to our manhood than usual. She shook her hard white finger near our faces and said that for very little she would write to our father and complain of our actions.

"Now," she said, in conclusion, "give your faces and hands a thorough washing and comb your hair, which is disgraceful; then come quietly down to tea." The door closed behind her.

"What beats me," said Angel, lathering his hands, "is why that wart on her chin wiggles so when she jaws us! I can't keep my eyes off it."

"It wiggles," piped The Seraph, as he dragged a brush over his curls, "'cos it's nervous, an' I wiggle when she scolds too, 'cos I'm nervous."

"Don't you worry, old man," Angel responded, gaily, "we'll take care of you."

We were in fine spirits despite our scolding. Indeed, we almost pitied Mrs. Handsomebody for her ignorance of the wonders amongst which she had her being.

Here she was, fussing over some stuffed birds in a glass case, when a live starling, who could talk, had perched near her very window sill! She spent hours in conversation with her Unitarian minister, while a real pirate lived next door.

It was pitiful, and yet it was very funny. We found it hard to go quietly down to tea with such thoughts in our minds, and after five hours in our bedroom.

IV

The next day was Sunday.

As we sat at dinner with Mrs. Handsomebody after morning service, we were scarcely conscious of the large, white dumplings that bulged before us, with a delicious sticky sweet sauce, trickling down their dropsical sides. We plied our spoons with languid interest around their outer edges, as calves nibble around a straw stack. Our vagrant minds scoured the Spanish Main with Captain Pegg.

Suddenly The Seraph spoke in that cock-sure way of his.

"There's a piwate at Peggs."

Mrs. Handsomebody looked at him sharply.

"What's that?" she demanded. At the same instant Angel and I kicked him under cover of the table.

"What did you say?" repeated Mrs. Handsomebody sternly.

"Funny ole gennelman at the Cwibbage Peggs," replied The Seraph with his mouth full.

Mrs. Handsomebody greatly respected Mr. and Mrs. Mortimer Pegg, and this play of words on the name incensed her.

"Am I to understand Alexander," she gobbled, "that you are making game of the Mortimer Peggs?"

"Yes," giggled the wretched Seraph, "it's a cwibbage game. You play it wiv Peggs."

"Leave the table instantly!" ordered Mrs. Handsomebody. "You are becoming unbearable."

The Seraph cast one anguished look at his dumpling and burst into

13

tears. We could hear his wails growing ever fainter as he plodded up the stairs.

"Mary Ellen, remove that dumpling!" commanded Mrs. Handsomebody.

Angel and I began to eat very fast. There was a short silence; then Mrs. Handsomebody said didactically:

"The elder Mr. Pegg is a much travelled gentleman, and one of the most noted archæologists of the day. A trifle eccentric in his manner perhaps but a deep thinker. David, can you tell me what an archæologist is?"

"Something you pretend you are," said Angel, "and you ain't."

"Nonsense!" snapped Mrs. Handsomebody. "Look it up in your Johnson's when you go upstairs, and let me know the result. I will excuse you now."

We found The Seraph lounging in a chair in the schoolroom.

"Too bad about the dumpling, old boy," I said consolingly.

"Oh, not too bad," he replied. "Mary Ellen fetched it up the backstairs to me. I'm vewy full."

That afternoon we saw Captain Pegg go for a walk with his son and daughter-in-law. He looked quite altered in a long grey coat and tall hat. Mr. and Mrs. Mortimer Pegg seemed proud to walk with him.

The following day was warm and sunny. When lessons were over we rushed to our bedroom window and to our joy we found that the window opposite was wide open, the wicker cage on the sill with the starling inside swelling up and preening himself in the sunshine, while just beyond sat Captain Pegg smoking a long pipe.

He seemed delighted to see us.

"Avast, my hearties!" he cried. "It's glorious sailing weather, but I've just been lying at anchor here, on the chance of sighting you. It does my heart good, y'see, to talk with some of my own kind, and leave off pretending to be an archæologist—to stretch my mental legs, as it were. Well—have you taken your bearings this morning?"

"Captain Pegg," I broke out with my heart tripping against my

14

blouse, "you said something the other day about buried treasure. Did you really find some? And would you mind telling us how you set about it?"

"Yes," he replied meditatively, "many a sack of treasure trove I've unearthed—but the most curious find of all, I got without searching and without blood being spilt. I was lying quiet those days, about forty years ago, off the north of the Orkney islands. Well, one morning I took a fancy to explore some of the outlying rocks and little islands dotted here and there. So I started off in a yawl with four seamen to row me; and not seeing much but barren rocks and stunted shrubs about, I bent over the stern and stared into the sea. It was as clear as crystal.

"As we were passing through a narrow channel between two rock islands, I bade the men rest on their oars, for something strange below had arrested my attention. I now could see plainly, in the green depths, a Spanish galleon, standing upright, held as in a vice, by the grip of the two great rocks. She must have gone down with all hands, when the greater part of the Spanish Armada was wrecked on the shores of Britain.

"'Shiver my timbers, lads,' I cried. 'Here'll be treasure in earnest! Back to the ship for our diving suits—booty for everyone, and plum duff for dinner!'

"Well, to make a long story short, I, and four of the trustiest of the crew, put on our diving suits, and soon we were walking the slippery decks once trodden by Spanish grandees and soldiers, and the scene of many a bloody fight I'll be bound. Their skeletons lay about the deck, wrapped in sea-tangle, and from every crevice of the galleon, tall, red, and green, and yellow, and purple weeds had sprung, that waved and shivered with the motion of the sea. Her decks were strewn with shells and sand, and in and out of her rotted ribs frightened fish darted at our approach. It was a gruesome sight.

"Three weeks we worked, carrying the treasure to our own ship, and I began to feel as much at home under water as above it. At last we set sail without mishap, and every man on board had his share and some of them gave up pirating and settled down as inn-keepers and tradesmen."

As the sound of his deep voice ceased, we three were silent also, gazing longingly into his eyes that were so like the sea.

15

Then—"Captain Pegg," said Angel, in a still, small voice, "I don't—s'pose—you'd know of any hidden treasure hereabouts? We'd most awfully like to find some. It'd be a jolly thing to write and tell father!"

A droll smile flickered over the bronzed features of Captain Pegg. He brought down his fist on the window-sill.

"Well, if you aren't chaps after my own heart!" he cried. "Treasure about here? I was just coming to that—and a most curious happening it is! There was a cabin-boy—name of Jenks—a lad that I trusted and loved like my own son, who stole the greater part of my share of the treasure, and, though I scoured the globe for him—" the Captain's eyes rolled fiercely—"I found neither trace of him nor the treasure, till two years ago. It was in Madagascar that I received a message from a dying man, confessing that, shaken by remorse, he had brought what was left of the plunder and buried it in Mrs. Handsomebody's back yard!"

"Mrs. Handsomebody's back yard!" We chanted the words in utter amazement.

"Just that," affirmed Captain Pegg solemnly. "Jenks found out that I owned the house next door but he dared not bury the treasure there because the yard was smoothly sodded, and would show up any disturbance; while Mrs. Handsomebody's yard, being covered with planks, was just the thing. So he simply raised one of the planks, dug a hole, and deposited the sack containing the last of the treasure, and wrote me his confession. And there you are!"

He smiled benignly on us. I longed to hug him.

The March wind swooped and whistled down the alley, and the starling gave little sharp twittering noises and cocked his head.

"When, oh when—" we burst out—"tonight? May we search for it tonight, Captain Pegg?"

He reflected. "No-o. Not tonight. Jenks, you see, sent me a plan of the yard with a cross to mark where the treasure lies, and I'll have to hunt it up so as not to waste our time turning up the whole yard. But tomorrow night—yes, tomorrow at midnight we'll start the search!"

V

At dinner that day the rice pudding had the flavor of ambrosia. By nightfall preparations were already on foot.

Firstly the shovel had been smuggled from the coal cellar and secreted in a corner of the yard behind the ash barrel together with an iron crowbar to use as a lever and an empty sack to aid in the removal of the treasure.

I scarcely slept that night, and when I did my mind was filled with wild imaginings. The next morning we were heedless scholars indeed, and at dinner I ate so little that Mrs. Handsomebody was moved to remark jocularly that somebody not a thousand miles away was shaping for a bilious bout.

At four o'clock Captain Pegg appeared at his window looking the picture of cheerful confidence. He said it warmed his heart to be at his old profession again, and indeed I never saw a merrier twinkle in any one's eyes. He had found the plan of the yard sent by Jenks and he had no doubt that we should soon be in possession of the Spanish treasure.

"But there's one thing, my lads;" he said solemnly, "I make no claim whatever to any share in this booty. Let that be understood. Anything we find is to be yours entirely. If I were to take any such goods into my son's house, his wife would get suspicious, uncomfortable questions would be asked, and it'd be all up with this archæologist business."

"Couldn't you hide it under your bed?" I suggested.

"Oh, she'd be sure to find it," he replied sadly. "She's into everything. And even if they didn't locate it till I am dead, they'd feel disgraced to think their father had been a pirate. You'll have to take it."

We agreed, therefore, to ease him of the responsibility of his strangely gotten gain. We then parted with the understanding that we were to meet him in the passage between the two houses promptly at midnight, and that in the meantime we were to preserve a calm and commonplace demeanour.

With the addition of four crullers and a slab of cold bread pudding filched from the pantry, our preparations were now complete.

17

We were well disciplined little animals; we always went to bed without a murmur, but on this night we literally flew there. The Seraph ended his prayers with—"and for this piwate tweasure make us twuly thankful. Amen."

The next moment we had dived under the bed clothes and snuggled there in wild expectancy.

From half past seven to twelve is a long stretch. The Seraph slept peacefully. Angel or I rose every little while and struck a match to look at the clock. At nine we were so hungry that we ate all four crullers. At eleven we ate the slab of cold bread pudding. After that we talked less, and I think Angel dozed, but I lay staring in the direction of the window, watching for the brightness which would signify that Captain Pegg was astir and had lighted his gas.

At last it came—a pale and trembling messenger, that showed our little room to me in a new aspect—one of mystery and grotesque shadows.

I was on my feet in an instant. I shook Angel's shoulder.

"Up with you!" I whispered, hoarsely. "The hour has come!"

I knew that drastic measures must be taken with The Seraph, so I just grasped him under the armpits and stood him on his feet without a word. He wobbled for a space, digging his knuckles in his eyes.

The hands of the clock pointed to ten minutes to twelve.

Angel and I hastily pulled on our trousers; and he, who liked to dress the part, stuck a knife in his belt, and twisted a scarlet silk handkerchief (borrowed from Mary Ellen) round his head. His dark eyes glistened under its folds.

The Seraph and I went unadorned, save that he girt his trusty sword about his stout middle and I carried a toy bayonet.

Down the inky-black stairs we crept, scarcely breathing. The lower hall seemed cavernous. I could smell the old carpets and the haircloth covering of the chairs. We sidled down the back hall among goloshes, umbrellas, and Turk's Head dusters. The back door had a key like that of a gaol.

Angel tried it with both hands, but though it grated horribly, it stuck. Then I had a try, and could not resist a triumphant click of the tongue when it turned, for Angel was a vain fellow and took a rise out of being the elder.

And when the moonlight shone upon us in the yard!—oh, the delicious freedom of it! We hopped for joy.

In the passage we awaited our leader. Between the roofs we could see the low half-moon, hanging like a tilted bird's nest in the dark blue sky, while a group of stars fluttered near it like young birds. The Cathedral clock sounded the hour of midnight.

Soon we heard the stealthy steps of Captain Pegg, and we gasped as we saw him, for in place of his flowered dressing-gown, he wore breeches and top boots, a loose shirt with a blue neckerchief knotted at the throat, and, gleaming at his side, a cutlass.

He smiled broadly when he saw us.

"Well, if you aren't armed—every man-jack of you—even to the bantling!" he cried. "Capital!"

"My sword, she's weal," said The Seraph with dignity. "Sometimes I fight giants."

Captain Pegg then shook hands with each of us in turn, and we thrilled at being treated as equals by such a man.

"And now to work!" he said heartily. "Here is the plan of the yard as sent by Jenks."

We could see it plainly by the moonlight, all neatly drawn out, even to the ash barrel and the clothes dryer, and there, on the fifth plank from the end was a cross in red ink, and beside it the magic word—Treasure!

Captain Pegg inserted the crowbar in a wide crack between the fourth and fifth boards, then we all pressed our full weight upon it with a "Yo heave ho, my hearties!" from our chief.

The board flew up and we flew down, sprawling on the ground. Somehow the Captain, versed in such matters, kept his feet, though he staggered a bit.

Then, in an instant, we were pulling wildly at the plank to dislodge it. This we accomplished after much effort, and a dark, dank recess was disclosed.

Captain Pegg dropped to his knees and with his hand explored cautiously under the planks. His face fell.

"Shiver my timbers if I can find it!" he muttered.

"Let me try!" I cried eagerly.

Both Angel and I thrust our hands in also and fumbled among the moist lumps of earth. I felt an earth-worm writhe away.

Captain Pegg now lighted a match and held it in the aperture. It cast a glow upon our tense faces.

"Hold it closer!" implored Angel. "This way—right here—don't you see?"

At the same moment we both had seen the heavy metal ring that projected, ever so little, above the surface of the earth. We grasped it simultaneously and pulled. Captain Pegg lighted another match. It was heavy—oh, so heavy!—but we got it out—a fair-sized leather bag bound with thongs. To one of these was attached the ring we had first caught sight of.

Now, kneeling as we were, we stared up in Captain Pegg's face. His wide, blue eyes had somehow got a different look.

"Little boys," he said gently, "open it!"

There in the moonlight, we unloosed the fastenings of the bag and turned its contents out upon the bare boards. The treasure lay disclosed then, a glimmering heap, as though, out of the dank earth, we had digged a patch of moonshine.

We squatted on the boards around it, our heads touching, our wondering eyes filled with the magic of it.

"It is the treasure," murmured Angel, in an awe-struck voice, "real treasure-trove. Will you tell us, Captain Pegg, what all these things are?"

Captain Pegg, squatting like the rest of us, ran his hands meditatively through the strange collection.

"Why, strike me purple," he growled, "if that scamp Jenks hasn't kept most of the gold coins and left us only the silver! But here's three golden doubloons, all right, one apiece for ye! And here's ducats and silver florins, and pieces of eight—and some I can't name till I get the daylight on them. It's a pretty bit of treasure all told; and see here—" he held up two old Spanish watches, just the thing for gentlemen adventurers.

We boys were now delving into the treasure on our own account, and brought to light a brace of antiquated pistols, an old silver flagon, a compass, a wonderful set of chess men carved from ivory, and some curious shells, that delighted The Seraph. And other quaint things there were that we handled reverently, and coins of different countries, square and round, and some with holes bored through.

We were so intent upon our discovery that none of us heard the approaching footsteps till they were fair upon us. Then, with a start, we turned, and saw to our horror Mrs. Handsomebody and Mary Ellen, with her hair in curl-papers, and, close behind them, Mr. and Mrs. Mortimer Pegg, scantily attired, the gentleman carrying a revolver.

"David! John! Alexander!" gobbled Mrs. Handsomebody.

"Now what d'ye think of that!" came from Mary Ellen.

"Father! Have you gone quite mad?" cried Mrs. Pegg.

And—"Oh, I say Governor—" stammered the gentleman with the revolver.

Captain Pegg rose to his feet with dignity.

"These young gentlemen," he said, simply, "have with my help been able to locate some buried treasure, stolen from me years ago by a man named Jenks, and hidden here since two decades. I hereby renounce all claim to it in favour of my three brave friends!"

Mr. Pegg was bent over the treasure.

"Now, look here, sir," he said, rather sharply, "some of this seems to be quite valuable stuff—"

"I know the value of it to a penny," replied his father, with equal asperity, "and I intend it shall belong solely and wholly to these boys."

"Whatever are you rigged up like that for?" demanded his daughter-in-law.

"As gentlemen of spirit," replied Captain Pegg, patiently, "we chose to dress the part. We do what we can to keep a little glamour and gaiety in the world. Some folk—" he looked at Mrs. Handsomebody—"would like to discipline it all away."

"I think," said our governess, "that, considering it is my back yard, I have some claim to—"

"None at all, Madam—none at all!" interrupted Captain Pegg. "By all the rules of treasure-hunting, the finder keeps the treasure."

Mrs. Handsomebody was silenced. She did not wish to quarrel with the Peggs.

Mrs. Pegg moved closer to her.

"Mrs. Handsomebody," she said, winking her white eyelashes very fast, "I really do not think that you should allow your pupils to accept this—er—treasure. My father-in-law has become very eccentric of late, and I am positive that he himself buried these things very recently. Only day before yesterday, I saw that set of ivory chessmen on his writing table."

"Hold your tongue, Sophia!" shouted Captain Pegg loudly.

Mr. Mortimer Pegg looked warningly at his wife.

"All right, Governor! Don't you worry," he said taking his father's arm. "It shall be just as you say; but one thing is certain, you'll take your death of cold if you stay out in this night air." As he spoke, he turned up the collar of his coat.

Captain Pegg shook hands grandly with Angel and me, then he lifted The Seraph in his arms and kissed him.

"Good-night, bantling," he said, softly. "Sleep tight!"

He turned then to his son. "Mort," said he, "I haven't kissed a little boy like that since you were just so high."

Mr. Pegg laughed and shivered, and they went off quite amiably, arm in arm, Mrs. Pegg following, muttering to herself.

Mrs. Handsomebody looked disparagingly at the treasure. "Mary Ellen," she ordered, "help the children to gather up that rubbish, and come in at once. Such an hour it is!"

Mary Ellen, with many exclamations, assisted in the removal of the treasure to our bedroom. Mrs. Handsomebody, after seeing it deposited there, and us safely under the bed-clothes, herself extinguished the gas.

"I shall write to your father," she said, severely, "and tell him the whole circumstance. Then we shall see what is to be done with you, and with the treasure."

With this veiled threat she left us. We snuggled our little bodies together. We were cold.

"I'll write to father myself, tomorrow, an' 'splain everything," I announced.

"D' you know," mused Angel, "I b'lieve I'll be a pirate, 'stead of a civil engineer like father. I b'lieve there's more in it."

"I'll be an engineer just the same," said I.

"I fink," murmured The Seraph, sleepily, "I fink I'll jus' be a bishop, an' go to bed at pwoper times an' have poached eggs for tea."

Chapter II

The Jilt

I

The day after the finding of the Treasure, Mary Ellen told us that she had seen Captain Pegg drive away from his son's house in a closed cab, before we had emerged from the four-poster. There had been a quarrel, the servants had told her, and in spite of all his son and daughter-in-law could do, the peppery Captain had left them, refusing to divulge the name of his destination.

"And they do say," Mary Ellen declared, "that he's no more fit to be wanderin' about the world alone than a babe unborn."

We smiled at the ignorance of women-servants, and speculated much on the Captain's probable new adventure. We were confident that he would return one day, loaded with fresh booty, and full of tales of the sea.

In the meantime, there was the Bishop. His house, as I have said stood between us and the Cathedral. It was a benign house, like a sleepy mastiff, and seemed to tolerate with lazy indifference the presence of its two narrow, high-backed neighbours, which with their cold, unblinking windows, looked like sinister, half-fed cats.

We had not been long at Mrs. Handsomebody's before we made friends with Bishop Torrance. As he walked in his deep, green garden, one morning, we three watched him enviously over the brick wall, that separated us. We were balanced precariously on a board, laid across the ash barrel, and The Seraph, losing his balance, fell headlong into a bed of clove pinks, almost at the Bishop's feet.

When his yells had subsided and explanations asked, and given, Angel and I were lifted over the wall, and shaken hands with, and given the freedom of the garden. We were introduced to the Bishop's niece, Margery, who was his sole companion, though we regarded, as one of the family, the Fountain Boy who blew cool jets of water through a shell, and turned his laughing face always upward toward the spires of the Cathedral.

24

Thus a quaint friendship sprang up, and, though the Bishop had not the dash, and boldness of Captain Pegg, he was an understanding and high-hearted playfellow.

I think The Seraph was his favourite. Even then, the dignified elegance of the Bishop's life appealed to that infant's love of the comfortable, and it tickled the Bishop immensely to have him pace solemnly up and down the garden, at his side, hands clasped behind his back, helping, as he believed, to "pwepare" the Bishop's sermon.

All three of us were permitted by Mrs. Handsomebody to join the Cathedral choir.

II

Thus we had a feeling of proprietorship in the Bishop and his garden, and his niece, Margery, and the Fountain Boy. Hence what was our astonishment and chagrin to see one morning, from our schoolroom window, a chit of a girl, smaller than myself, strutting up and down the Bishop's garden, pushing a doll's perambulator. She had fluffy golden hair about her shoulders, and her skirts gave a rhythmic swing as she turned the corners. Now and then she would stop in her walk, remove the covering from the doll, do some idiotic thing to it, and replace the cover with elaborate care.

We stared fascinated. Then Angel blew out his lips in disgust, and said—

"Ain't girls the most sickenin' things?"

"There she goes again, messing with the doll's quilt," I agreed.

"Le's fwow somefing at her!" suggested The Seraph.

"Yes, and get into a row with the Bishop," answered Angel. "But I don't see myself going over there to play again. She's spoiled everything."

"I s'pose she's a spoiled child," said The Seraph, dreamily. "Wonder where her muvver is."

"I say," said Angel, "let's rap on the pane, and then when she looks up, we'll all stick our tongues out at her. That'll scare her all right!"

We did.

When her wondering blue eyes were raised to our window, what they saw was three white disks pressed against the glass, with a flattened pink tongue protruding from each. We glared to see the effect of this outrage upon her. But the dauntless little creature never quailed. Worse than that, she put her fingers to her lips and blew three kisses at us—one apiece.

We were staggered. We withdrew our reddened faces hastily and stared at each other. We were aghast. Almost we had been kissed by a girl!

"Let's draw the blind!" said Angel. "She shan't see us! Then we can peek through the crack and watch her."

But no sooner was the blind pulled down than we heard our governess coming and flew to our seats.

"Boys!" she gobbled, stopping in the doorway, "what does this mean? The boy who pulled down that blind stand up!"

Angel rose. "The light hurt my eyes," he lied feebly, "I aren't very well."

"Ridiculous!" snapped Mrs. Handsomebody, running up the blind with precision, "this room at its brightest is dim. Your eyes are keen enough for mischief, sir. Now we shall proceed with our arithmetic."

We floundered through the Tables, but my mind still wandered in the Bishop's garden. Resentment and curiosity struggled for mastery within me. In my mind's eye I saw her covering and uncovering the doll. Why did she do it? What did it feel like to push that "pram"? Would she drink tea from the Indian Tree cups and be allowed to strum on the piano? Oh, I wished she hadn't come! And yet—anyway, I was glad I was a boy.

As Fate had it, Angel and The Seraph had to have their hair trimmed that afternoon. My own straight blond crop grew but slowly so I was free for an hour to follow my own devices. Those led me to climb to the roof of our scullery and from there mount the high brick wall.

From this vantage point I scanned the surrounding country for signs of the interloper. There she was! There she was!

Down on her knees at the fountain's brink, her curls almost touching the water, she was sailing boats made of hollyhock petals. The doll's perambulator stood near by.

Noiselessly I crept along the wall till I reached the cherry tree that stood in the corner. Reaching its friendly branches, I let myself down, hand over hand, till, at last, I dropped lightly on the soft turf.

I sauntered then to her side, and gazed at her moodily. If she saw me she gave no sign.

In spite of myself I grew interested in the way she manipulated those boat petals. Evidently there was some system in her game but it was new to me.

"That little black seed on this boat is Jason," she said at last, without looking up, "and these little white seeds are his comrades. They're searching for The Golden Fleece. My hair is the Fleece. Come and play!"

Mutely I squatted beside her, and our two faces peered at each other in the mirror of the pool.

She gave a funny eager little laugh.

"Oh," she cried, "we match beautifully, don't we? Your hair is yellow and my hair is yellow, my eyes are blue and your eyes are blue."

"My eyes are grey, like father's," I objected.

"No, they're blue like mine. We match beautifully. Let's play something else." Before I could prevent her, she had swept Jason and his crew away, and, snatching the doll from the perambulator, had set it on the fountain's edge between us.

"This is Dorothea," she announced, "isn't she sweet? I'm her mother. You should be the father, and Dorothea should want to paddle her toes in the fountain. Now you hold her—so."

Before I was aware of it I was made to grasp the puppet by the waist, while her mistress began to rearrange the pillows in the "pram."

I glanced fearfully at our schoolroom window, lest I should be discovered in so unmanly a posture. It seemed that we were quite alone and unobserved.

A drowsy pleasure stole over my senses. The humming of the bees in the Canterbury Bells became a chant as of sirens. Dorothea's silly pink feet dangled in the pool. Surreptitiously I slipped my hand under water and felt them. They were getting spongy and seemed likely to come off. Truly there were compensations for such slavery.

My companion returned and sat down with her slim body close to mine.

"What is your name?" she cooed.

"John."

"Oh. Mine is Jane. You may call me Jenny. I'm visiting Aunt Margery. The Bishop is my great-uncle. What are your brothers' names?"

"Angel and The Seraph. They don't like girls." Instantly I wondered why I had said that. Did I like girls? Not much. But I didn't want Angel interfering in this. He had better keep away.

"My father is a judge. He sends bad men to prison."

"My father"—I was very proud of him—"is a civil engineer. He's in South America building a railroad, so that's why we live with Mrs. Handsomebody. But some day he's coming back to make a home for us. When I grow up I shall be an engineer too, and build bridges over canyons."

"What's canyons? Hold Dorothea tighter."

I explained canyons at length.

"P'raps I'll take you with me," I added weakly.

She clapped her hands rapturously.

"Oh, what fun!" she gurgled. "I can keep house and hang my washing 'cross the canyon to dry!"

Frankly I did not relish the thought of my canyon's being thus desecrated. I determined never to allow her to do any such thing, but, at the moment I was willing to indulge her fancy.

"Yes," she prattled on, "I'll wheel Dorothea up and down the bridge and watch you work."

Now there was some sense in that. What man does not enjoy being admired while he does things? In fact Jane had hit upon a great elemental truth when she suggested this. From that moment I was hers.

Laying Dorothea, toes up, on the grass I proceeded to lead Jane into the most cherished realms of my fancy. Together we sailed those "perilous seas in faery lands forlorn," dabbling our hands in the fountain, while the golden August sunshine kissed our necks.

I said not a word of this at tea. I munched my bread and butter in a sort of haze, scarcely conscious of the subdued conversation led by Mrs. Handsomebody, until I heard her say,

"A little great-niece of Bishop Torrance is visiting next door. You are therefore invited to take tea with her tomorrow afternoon. I trust you will conduct yourselves with decency at table, and remember that a frail little girl is not to be played with as a headlong boy."

I felt that she couldn't tell me anything about frail little girls, but I kept my knowledge to myself. The Seraph said—

"Was you ever a fwail little gel, Mrs. Handsomebody?" Our governess fixed him with her eye.

"I was a most decorous and obedient little girl, Alexander, and asked no impertinent questions of my elders."

"Was Mary Ellen a fwail little gel?" persisted The Seraph.

"No," snapped Mrs. Handsomebody, "judging from her characteristics as a servant, I should say that she was a very riotous, rude little girl. Now drink your milk."

"I yike wiotous wude people," said The Seraph with his face in the tumbler; the milk trickled down his chin.

"Leave the table, Alexander," commanded Mrs. Handsomebody, "your conduct is quite inexcusable." The Seraph departed, weeping.

All that evening I thought about Jane. I had no heart for a pillow fight. At night I dreamed of her, and saw her weekly washing, suspended from a line, fluttering in the wind that raced along my canyon.

I strained toward the hour when I should meet her at tea. I had never felt like this before. True, I had once conceived a violent fancy for a fat young woman in the pastry shop, but she had been replaced by a thin young woman who did not appeal to me, and the episode was forgotten.

But, oh, this bitter-sweetness of my love for Jane! My despair when I found that she was to sit next Angel at tea, till I discovered that, seated opposite, I could stare at her, and admire how she nibbled her almond cake and sipped tea from an apple-green cup.

After tea we played musical chairs, in the library, with Margery at the piano. First marched The Seraph with his brown curls bobbing; and after him, the stout Bishop in his gaiters; next Angel; then Jane on tiptoes; and lastly myself in squeaky new boots.

Seraph and the Bishop were soon out of it. They were invariably beaten in our games, though afterward they always seemed to think they had won. So Angel, Jane, and I were left, prancing around two solemn carved chairs. The music ceased with a crash. Jane leaped to one chair while Angel and I fell simultaneously upon the other. We both clung to it desperately, but he dislodged me, inch by inch, and I, furious at being balked in my pursuit of Jane, struck him twice in the ribs, then ran into the dim hall and hid myself.

There Jane found me, and there her tender lips kissed my hot cheek, and she squeezed me in her arms. For a moment we did not speak, then she whispered—

"I wish you had got the chair, John. I love you best of all."

That night I hung about the kitchen while Mary Ellen was setting bread to rise. The time had come when I must speak to some fellow creature of this tremendous new element that had come into my life. I watched Mary Ellen's stout red arms as she manipulated the dough, in much perplexity. The kitchen was hot, the kettle sang, it seemed a moment for confidence, yet words were hard to find.

At last I got out desperately:

"Mary Ellen, what is love like?"

"Love is it, Masther John? What do the likes o' me know about love thin?" She smiled broadly, as she dexterously shifted the puffy white mass.

"Oh, you know," I persisted, "'cos you've been in it, often. You've had lots of 'followers' now, Mary Ellen, haven't you?"

"Well, thin, if ye must know, I'll tell ye point blunt to kape out av it. It's an awful thing whin it gits the best av ye."

"But what's it feel like?" I probed.

Mary Ellen wiped the flour off each red finger in turn, and gazed into the flame of the lamp.

"It's like this," she said solemnly, "ye burns in yer insides till ye feel like ye had a furnace blazin' there. Thin whin it seems ye must bust wid the flarin' av it, ye suddintly turns cowld as ice, an' yer sowl do shrivil up wid fear. An' thin, at last, ye fergit all about it till the nixt wan happens along. Och—I haven't had a sphell fer months! This is an awful dull place. I think I'll be quittin' it soon."

"Oh, no, no, Mary Ellen!" I cried, alarmed, "you mustn't leave us! When Jane and I get married you can come and live with us." I blushed furiously.

"And who might Jane be?" demanded Mary Ellen, suspiciously.

"She's the Bishop's great-niece," I explained proudly. "I love her terribly, Mary Ellen. It hurts in here." I pressed my hand on my stomach.

"Well, well." She shook her head commiseratingly. "I'm sorry fer ye, Masther John—sthartin' off like this at your age. Here's the spoon I stirred the cake wid—have a lick o' that. It'll mebbe help ye."

I licked pensively at the big wooden spoon, and felt strangely soothed. My admiration for Mary Ellen increased.

As I slowly climbed the stairs for bed, visions of Jane hovered in the darkness above me—airy rainbows, with Jane's laughing face peering between the bars of pink and gold. I had never known a little girl before, and Jane embodied all things frail and exquisite.

When I entered our room Angel was sitting on the side of the bed, pulling his shirt over his head. The Seraph already slept in his place next the wall.

I stood before Angel with folded arms.

31

"Hm," he muttered crossly, "you've been lickin' batter! It's on the end of your nose. Why didn't you get me something?"

"There was nothing but dough," I explained, "and one batter spoon. And—and—I say, Angel—"

"Well?" asked my elder tersely.

"I—I'm in love something awful. It hurts. It's like this—" I hurried on—"You feel like you'd a furnace blazing in you, an' then you turn cold jus' as if you'd shrivel up, but you never, never, forget, an'—It's made a 'normous difference in my life, Angel—"

I got no further. Angel had thrown himself backward on the bed and, kicking his bare legs in the air, broke into peals of delighted laughter.

"It's that yellow-faced little Jenny!" he gurgled, "Oh, holy smoke!"

His brutal mirth was short-lived. Mrs. Handsomebody appeared in the doorway, her face genuinely shocked at the sight that met her austere eyes.

At this hour—such actions—was her house to be turned into Bedlam?—such indecent display of limbs—she was sick with shame for Angel—would discuss his conduct further, with him, tomorrow.

She waited while I undressed and stood over us while we said our prayers at the side of the bed, at last extinguishing the light with a final admonition to be silent.

I was bitterly disappointed in Angel. It was the first time he had failed me utterly. I put my arms around the sleeping Seraph and cried myself to sleep.

III

We were awakened by the sonorous music of the Cathedral chimes. It was Sunday. That meant stiff white Eton collars, and texts gabbled between mouthfuls of porridge; and, later, our three small bodies arrayed in short surplices, and the long service in the Cathedral. The Seraph was the very smallest boy in the choir. I think he was only tolerated there through Margery's intervention, because it would have broken his loyal little heart to be separated from Angel and me. He was highly ornamental too, as he collected the choir offertory in a little velvet bag, his tiny surplice jauntily bobbing, and the back of his neck, as an old lady once said, was more touching than the sermon.

Angel had a voice like a flute.

Beyond the tall choir stalls I could catch fleeting glimpses of Jane's little face beneath her daisied hat, looking on the same prayer-book with Margery. I swelled my chest beneath my surplice and chanted my very loudest in the hope that Jane might hear me. "O ye Showers and Dew, bless ye the Lord: praise him, and magnify him for ever."

Her dreamy blue eyes peered over the edge of the book, the daisies on her hat nodded; she smiled; I smiled ecstatically back at her; and so two childish hearts stemmed the flood of praise that rose above the old grey pillars.

At dinner, over his bread pudding, The Seraph murmured in a throaty voice—"When you is in love, first you burns yike a furnace, an' en you shwivel up wiv the cold. It's a vewy bad fing to be in love."

I threw Angel a bitter look. This was his doing. So, contemptuously, had he treated my confidence, made as man to man. To tell the irresponsible Seraph of all people!

"What's that, Alexander?" questioned Mrs. Handsomebody, sharply.

"It's love," replied The Seraph, meekly, "you catch it off a girl. John's got it."

Mrs. Handsomebody sank back in her chair with a groan.

"Alexander," she said it solemnly, "I tremble for your future. You are not the boy your father was. I tremble for you."

"John," she continued, turning to me, "you will come into the parlour with me. I wish to have a talk with you. David and Alexander, you may amuse yourselves with one of my bound volumes of 'The Quiver.'"

I followed her with burning cheeks into the stiff apartment where not only her eye was riveted upon me, but every glittering eye of every stuffed bird, to say nothing of the pale fixed gaze of Mr. Handsomebody.

Needless to recall the lecture I received, the probing into my reluctant heart, the admonition which I could not heed for my fearful watching of that hard grey face.

But, at last, it was over. I slipped into the hall, closing the door softly behind me, and listened. Silence abounded. On tiptoe I made my way to the kitchen. It was clean and empty. I noiselessly opened the back door. On the doorstep sat The Seraph busily engaged with a caterpillar.

"Where's Angel?" I demanded curtly.

"I fink," breathed The Seraph, stroking the caterpillar the wrong way, and then looking at his fingers, "I fink that he's witin' to father to tell on you. So there!"

I waited to hear no more. Casting my care behind me I sped lightly along the passage between the houses, crossed the Bishop's lawn, and sought Jane in the garden.

There I stood a moment, dazzled, by the golden August sunshine, the iridescent spray of the fountain, and the brilliant colours of the hollyhocks beside the wall.

I saw Jane there, and my heart swelled with disappointment and rage—for she was not alone!

Too late I repented my confidence to Angel; I might have known that he would never let the grass grow under his feet till he had tasted this new excitement. Well, he had not let the grass grow.

Jane, I remember, had on a pale blue sash, and a fluffy white frock, beneath the frills of which, her slender black silk legs moved airily. By her side sauntered the traitorous Angel, his head bent toward her tenderly, and, most sickening of all, pushing before him, with an air of proprietorship, the perambulator containing the doll, Dorothea. Jane was simpering up at him in a way she had never looked at me.

I saw at a glance that all was over, yet I was not to be cast aside thus lightly. I strode across the garden, and, pushing myself between them, I laid my hand masterfully on the handle of the "pram," beside Angel's. Neither of them uttered a word. So the three of us walked for a space in tense silence.

Then, suddenly, Angel began to hammer my hand with his fist.

"You let go of that!" he snarled. "Ge—tout of here!"

"I won't!" I roared tragically. "She said I was the fa-ather of it!"

"She did not!" yelled Angel. "I'm the father!"

Jenny glanced fearfully at the windows of the Bishop's house. All was silent there. Then, with a scornful little kick at me, she said— "Go 'way, you nasty boy! I don't want you. I only like Angel."

There was nothing more to be said. I hung my head, and, with a sob in my throat, turned away. I could hear them whispering behind me.

Before I reached our own yard Angel came running after me.

"Tell you what I'll do, John," he said, as he came abreast, "tell you what I'll do—I'll fight you for her. Like knights of old, you know. We could go down to the coal cellar, and have a reg'lar tourney. It'd be bully fun. We could have pokers for lances. Say, will you?"

I was not in a fighting mood, but I had never refused a challenge, and, somehow, the thought of bloodshed eased my pain a little. So, half-reluctantly, I followed him, as he eagerly led the way to the coal cellar.

Even on this August day it was cold down there. Long cobwebs trailed, spectre-like from the beams, and a faint squeaking of young mice could be heard in the walls.

We searched among the débris of years for suitable weapons. Finally, brandishing pokers, and with two rusty boiler lids for shields, we faced each other, uttering our respective battle cries in muffled tones. Angel had put a battered coal scuttle over his head for a helmet; and, through a break in it, I could see his dark eyes gleaming threateningly.

With ring of shield we clashed together. I delivered—and received— stunning blows. Dust, long undisturbed, rose, and blinded us.

How many a gallant fray has been broken up by a screaming woman! Now Mary Ellen, true to the perversity of her sex, rushed in to separate us.

"Oh, losh! I never seen the beat o' ye!" she cried. "Ye've scairt me out av a year's growth! Sure the missus'll put a tin ear on ye, if she catches ye in the cellar in yer collars an' all!" Imperiously she disarmed us, and, without ceremony, we were hustled up the dark stairs to the kitchen sink.

"It was a tournament, Mary Ellen, about a lady," I explained, with as much dignity as I could muster, "you shouldn't have interrupted."

"There ain't a lady livin' that's worth messin' up yer clane clothes for," said Mary Ellen, sternly. "Lord! To see the cinders in yer hair, an' the soot in yer ears—it does bate all—" As she talked, she scrubbed us vehemently with a washcloth.

"Ouch!" moaned Angel, "oh, Mary El-len, you're hurting me! That's my so-ore spot, eeeoow!"

"Well, Master Angel," said Mary Ellen, "I don't want to hurt ye, but it do make me heart-sick to see ye bashin' aitch other wid pokers for the sake av a bit girl that's not worth a tinker's curse to ye! Now thin—here's a piece of cowld puddin' to each av ye—sit on the durestep where the missus won't see ye, an' git outside av it."

In a chastened mood we sat outside the back door and ate our pudding. It was cold, clammy, very sweet, and deliciously satisfying.

To our right the wall excluded any glimpse of the Bishop's garden, and beyond loomed the Cathedral, with two grey pigeons circling about its spire.

I yearned to know what was going on beyond the wall. I could not help fancying that Jane, touched by remorse, was weeping by the fountain for me, and me only. Angel spoke.

"I say—" he hunched his shoulders mischievously—"let's go 'round and see what she's doin' all alone, eh?"

I leaped to the proposal. I had an insatiable desire to hear her speak once more, if it were only to taunt me.

We made the passage stealthily; all the world seemed drowsing on that hazy Sunday afternoon. The blinds in the Bishop's study were drawn. Little did he guess the life his great-niece led!

The grass was like moist velvet beneath our feet. A pair of sparrows were quarrelling over their bath at the fountain rim. We heard a low murmur of voices. A glint of Jane's white frock could be seen behind a guelder rose near the fountain. We crept up behind and peered through the foliage.

There on a garden bench sat Jane, and there, clasped in her slim white arms was—The Seraph! The wretched Dorothea lay, face downward, on the grass at their feet.

We strained our ears to hear what was being said. Jane spoke in that silvery voice of hers:

"Say some more drefful things, Seraph. I jus' love to hear you."

There was a moment's silence; then, The Seraph said in his blandest tone, the one word—

"Blood!"

Jane gave a tiny, ecstatic shriek.

"Oh, go on!" she begged, "say more."

"Blood," repeated The Seraph, firmly, "Hot blood—told blood—wed blood—thick blood—thin blood—bad blood."

Again Jane squealed in fearful pleasure.

"Go on," she urged. "Worser."

Thus encouraged, The Seraph rapped out, without more ado, "Tiger blood—ephelant blood—caterpillar blood—ole witch blood"—then, after a pause, that the horror of it might sink deep in—"Baby blood!"

Angel and I gave each other a look of enlightenment. It was gore then, that this delicately nurtured young person craved, good red gore, and plenty of it! Well—enough—we were free. Wait! What was she saying?

"I hate those other boys, Seraph, darling. Let's jus' you and me play together always. And you should be Dorothea's father, and Dorothea should want to paddle in the—"

Away! Away! With sardonic laughter, we sped along the pebbled drive, nor stopped until we reached our own domain.

Then in the planked back yard, we sat on our steps, with a volume of "The Quiver" on our knees, in case Mrs. Handsomebody should invade our privacy, and played a rollicking game of pirates. And when any of the fair sex fell into our hands we were none too gentle with them.

"Chuck 'em overboard, lieutenant!" was Captain Angel's way of dealing with the case.

Just as the Cathedral clock struck five, The Seraph swaggered up. He stopped before us, hands deep in pockets.

"Well," said Angel, eyeing him resentfully, "you'll make a nice bishop, you will, usin' the language we heard a bit ago!"

"Maybe I shan't have time to be a bishop, after all," replied The Seraph, condescendingly. "You see I'm goin' to mawy Jane. It'll keep me vewy busy."

Chapter III

Explorers of the Dawn

I

Fast on the wingèd heels of Love came our discovery of the Dawn. Of course we had known all along that there was a sunrise—a mechanical sort of affair that started things going like clockwork. But Dawn was a bird of another feather.

If we had had our parents with us they would have, in all likelihood, unfolded the mystery of it in some bedtime visit; but Mrs. Handsomebody, if she ever thought about the Dawn at all, probably looked on it with suspicion, and some disfavour, as a weak, feeble thing—a nebulous period fit neither for honest folk nor cutthroats.

So it came about that we heard of it from our good friend the Bishop. Mrs. Handsomebody had given a grudging permission for us to take tea with him. In hot weather her voice and eyes always seemed frostier than usual. The closely shut windows and drawn blinds made the house a prison, and the glare of the planked back yard was even more intolerable. Therefore, when Rawlins, the Bishop's butler, told us that we were to have tea in the garden, it was hard for us to remember Mrs. Handsomebody's injunction to walk sedately and to bear in mind that our host was a bishop.

But, as we crossed the cool lawn, our spirits, which had drooped all day, like flags at half-mast, rose, and fluttered in the summer breeze, and we could not resist a caper or two as we approached the tea-table.

The Bishop did not even see us. His fine grave face was buried in a book he had on his knees, and his gaitered legs were bent so that he toed in.

When we drew up before him, Angel and I in stiff Eton collars and The Seraph fresh as a daisy, in a clean white sailor blouse, he raised his eyes and gave us a vague smile, and a wave of the hand toward three low wicker chairs. We were not a bit abashed by this reception, for we knew the Bishop's ways, and it was joy enough that we were safe in his garden staring up at the blue sky through

39

flickering leaves, and listening to the splash of the little fountain that lived in the middle of the cool grass plot.

Surely, I thought, there never was such another garden—never another with such a rosy red brick wall, half-hidden by hollyhocks and larkspur—such springy, tender grass—such a great guardian Cathedral, that towered above and threw its deep beneficent shade! Here the timorous Cathedral pigeons strutted unafraid, and dipped their heads to drink of the fountain, raising them Heavenward, as they swallowed—thanking God, so the Bishop said, for its refreshment.

It was hard to believe that next door, beyond the wall, lay Mrs. Handsomebody's planked back yard. Yet even at that moment I could see the tall, narrow house, and fancied that a blind moved as Mrs. Handsomebody peered down into the Bishop's garden to see how we behaved.

Rawlins brought a tray and set it on the wicker table beside the Bishop's elbow. We discovered a silver muffin dish, a plate of cakes, and a glass pot of honey, to say nothing of the tea.

Still the Bishop kept his gaze buried in his book, marking his progress with a blade of grass. Rawlins stole away without speaking and we three were left alone to stare in mute desire at the tea things. A bee was buzzing noisily about the honey jar. It was The Seraph who spoke at last, his hands clasped across his stomach.

"Bishop," he said, politely, but firmly. "I would yike a little nushment."

"Bless me!" cried the Bishop. "Wherever are my manners?" And he closed the book sharply on the grass blade, and dropped it under the table. "John, will you pour tea for us?"

We finished the muffins and cake, all talking with our mouths full, in the most sociable and sensible way; and, after the honey pot was almost empty, we made the bee a prisoner in it, so that, like that Duke of Clarence, who was drowned in a butt of Malmsey, he got enough of what he liked at last.

I think it was Angel who put the question that was to lead to so much that was exciting and mysterious.

He said, leaning against the Bishop's shoulder: "What do you think is the most beautiful thing in the world, Bishop?"

40

Our friend had The Seraph between his knees, and was gazing at the back of his head. "Well," he replied, "since you ask me seriously, I should say this little curl on The Seraph's nape."

The Seraph felt for it.

"I yike it," he said, "but I yike my wart better."

"Good gracious," exclaimed the Bishop. "Don't tell me you've a wart!"

"Yes, a weal one," chuckled The Seraph. "It's little, but it's gwowing. I fink some day it'll be as big as the one on Mrs. Handsomebody's chin. It can wiggle."

"You don't say so!" said the Bishop, rather hastily. "And where do you suppose you got it?"

The Seraph smiled mischievously. "I fink I got it off a toad we had. He was an awful dear ole toad, but he died, 'cos we—"

"Oh, I say, don't bother about the old toad, Seraph!" put in Angel hastily, feeling, as I did, that the manner of the toad's demise was best left to conjecture. "We want to hear about the most beautiful thing in the world. Please tell it, Bishop!"

"Well—since you corner me," said the Bishop, his eyes on the larkspur, "I should say it is the wing of that pale blue butterfly, hovering above those deep blue flowers."

Angel's face fell. "Oh, I didn't mean a little thing like that," he said. "I meant a 'normous, wonderful thing. Something that you couldn't ever forget."

"Well—if you will have it," said the Bishop, "come close and I'll whisper." Instantly three heads hedged him in, and he said in a sonorous undertone—"It's the Dawn."

"The Dawn!" We three repeated the magic words on the same note of secrecy. "But what is it like? How can we get to it? Is it like the sunset?"

"I won't explain a bit of it," he replied. "You've got to seek it out for yourselves. It's a pity, though, you can't see it first in the country."

"Must we get up in the dark?"

41

"Yes. I think your tallest attic window faces the east. You must steal up there while it's still grey daylight. Have the windows open so that you can hear and smell, as well as see it. But I'm afraid the dear Seraph's too little."

"Not me," asserted The Seraph, stoutly. "I'm stwong as two ephelants."

"You mustn't be frightened when you hear its wings," said the Bishop, "nor be abashed at the splendour of it, for it was designed for just such little fellows as you. You will come and tell me then what happens, won't you? I shall probably never waken early enough to see it again."...

II

Though we played games after this, and the Bishop made a very satisfactory lion prowling about in a jungle of wicker chairs and table legs, we none of us quite lost sight of the adventure in store for us. Somewhere in the back of our heads lurked the thought of the Dawn with its suggestion of splendid mystery.

We were no sooner at home again than we set about discussing ways and means.

"The chief thing," said Angel, "is to waken about four. We have no alarm clock, so I s'pose we'll just have to take turns in keeping watch all night. The hall clock strikes, so we can watch hour about."

"I'll take first watch!" put in The Seraph, eagerly.

"You'll take just what's given to you, and no questions, young man," said Angel, out of the side of his mouth, and The Seraph subsided, crushed.

Came bedtime at last, and the three of us in the big four-poster; the door shut upon the world of Mrs. Handsomebody, and the windows firmly barred against burglars and night air.

Angel announced: "First watch for me! You go right to sleep, John, and I'll wake you when the clock strikes ten. Then you'll feel nice and fresh for your watch."

But I wasn't at all sleepy and we lay in the dusk and talked till the familiar harsh voice of the hall clock rasped out nine o'clock.

"You go to sleep, please John," whispered Angel in a drowsy voice, "and I'll watch till ten."

I felt drowsy too, so I put my arm about the slumbering Seraph and soon fell fast asleep.

It seemed to me but a moment when Angel roused me. I know I had barely settled down to an enjoyable dream in which I was the only customer in an ice-cream parlour, where there were seven waitresses, each one obsequiously proffering a different flavour.

"Second watch on deck!" whispered Angel, hoarsely—"and look lively!"

"But I'd only just put my spoon in the strawberry ice," I moaned. "Can't be ten minutes yet."

"Oh, I say," complained Angel, "don't you s'pose I know when the old clock strikes ten? You've been sleepin' like a drunken pirate and no mistake. Must be near eleven by now."

"I'll just see for myself," I declared. "I'll go and look at the schoolroom clock." And I began to scramble over him.

"You will not then—" muttered Angel, clutching me. "I shan't let you!"

"You won't, eh? If it's really ten you needn't care, need you!"

"Course it's ten—It's nearer eleven, but you're going to do what I say."

At that we came to grips and fought and floundered till the bed rocked, and the poor little Seraph clung to his pillow as a shipwrecked sailor to a raft in a stormy sea. Exhaustion alone made us stop for breath; still we clung desperately to each other, our small bodies pressed hotly together, Angel's nose flattened against my ear. The Seraph snuggled up to us. "Just you wait"—breathed Angel—his hands tightened on me, then relaxed—his legs twitched— "Strawberry or pineapple, sir?" came the dulcet tones of the waitress. I was in my ice-cream parlour again! Seven flavours were laid before me. I fell to, for I was hot and thirsty.

43

I was disturbed by The Seraph, singing his morning song. It was a tuneless drone, yet not unmusical. Always the first to open his eyes in the morning, he began his day with a sort of Saga of his exploits of the day before, usually meaningless to us but fraught with colour from his own peculiar sphere. At last he laughed outright—a Jovian laugh—at some remembered prank—and I rubbed my eyes and came to full consciousness. The sun was slanting through the shutters. Where, oh where, was the Dawn?

I turned to look at Angel. He was staring at the slanting beam and swearing softly, as he well knew how.

"We'll simply have to try again"—I said. "But however are we going to put in today?"

The problem solved itself as all problems will and the day passed, following the usual landmarks of porridge, arithmetic, spelling, scoldings, mutton, a walk with our governess, bread and butter, prayers, and the (for once, longed for!) bed.

That night we decided to lie awake together; passing the time with stories, and speculation about the mystery so soon to be explored by us. I told the first story, a long-drawn adventure of shipwreck, mutiny and coral Caves, with a fair sprinkling of skeletons to keep us broad awake.

"It was a first-rate tale," sighed Angel, contentedly, when I had done, "an' you told it awfully well, John. If you like you may just tell another 'stead o' me. Or The Seraph can tell one. Go ahead, Seraph, and make up the best story you know how."

The Seraph, important, but sleepy, climbed over me, so that he might be in the middle, and then began, in a husky little voice:

"Once upon a time there was fwee bwothers, all vwey nice, but the youngest was the bwavest an' stwongest of the fwee. He was as stwong as two bulls, an' he'd kill a dwagon before bweakfast, an' never be cocky about it—"

Angel and I groaned in unison. We could not tolerate this sort of self-adulation from our junior. "Don't be such a little beast"—we admonished, and covered his head with a pillow. The Seraph was wont to accept such discipline, at our hands, philosophically, with no unseemly outcries or struggles; as a matter of fact, when we uncovered his head, we could tell by his even, reposeful breathing that he was fast asleep. It was too dark to see his face, but I could imagine his complacent smile.

The night sped quickly after that. There was some desultory talk; then Angel, too, slept; I resolved to keep the watch alone. I heard the sound of footsteps in the street below, echoing, with a lonely sound; the rattle of a loose shutter in a sudden gust of wind; then, dead silence, followed after an interval by the scampering, and angry squeak of mice in the wall....

The mice disturbed me again. There was a shattering of loose plaster; and suddenly opening my eyes, I saw the ghost of grey daylight stealing underneath the blind. The time had come!

III

Silently the three of us stole up the uncarpeted attic stair. It was unknown territory to us, having been forbidden from the first by Mrs. Handsomebody, and all we had ever seen from the hall below was a cramped passage, guarded by three closed doors. Time and time again we had been tempted to explore it, but there was a sinister aloofness about it that had hitherto repelled us. Now, however, it had become but a pathway to the Dawn, and, as we clutched the bannisters, we imagined ourselves three pilgrims fearfully climbing toward light and beauty.

Angel stood first at the top. Gently he tried two doors in succession, which were locked. The third gave, harshly—it seemed to me, grudgingly.

The Seraph and I pressed close behind Angel, glad of the warm contact of each other's bodies.

In the large attic room, the air was stifling, and the sloping roof, from which dim cobwebs were draped, seemed to press toward the dark shapes of discarded furniture as though to guard some fearful secret. It took all our courage to grope our way to the low casement, and it was a struggle to dislodge the rusty bolt, and press the window out on its unused hinges. It creaked so loudly that we held our breath for a moment, but we drew it again with a sharp sensation of relief, as thirsty young animals drink, for fresh night

45

air, sweet, stinging to the nostrils, had surged in upon us, sweeping away fear, and loneliness, and the hot depression of the attic room.

Mrs. Handsomebody's house was tall, and we could look down upon many roofs and chimneys. They huddled together in the soft grey light as though waiting for some great happening which they expected, but did not understand. They wore an air of expectancy and humility. Little low-roofed out-houses pressed close to high walls for shelter, and a frosty white skylight stared up-ward fearfully.

"Is this the Dawn?" came from The Seraph, in a tiny voice.

"Only the beginning of it," I whispered back. "There's two stars left over from the night—see! that big blue one in the east, and the little white one just above the cobbler's chimney."

"Will they be afwaid of the Dawn, when it comes?"

"Rather. I shouldn't be surprised if the big fellow bolted right across the sky, and the little one will p'raps fall down the cobbler's chimney into his work-room."

The Seraph was enchanted. "Then the cobbler'll sew him wight up in the sole of a shoe, an' the boy who wears the shoe will twinkle when he wuns, won't he? Oh, it's coming now! I hear it. I'm afwaid."

"That's not the Dawn," said Angel, "that's the night flying away."

It was true that there came to us then a rushing sound, as of strong wings; our hair was lifted from our hot foreheads; and the casement rattled on its hinges.

This wind, that came from the wings of night, was sharp with the fragrance of heather and the sea. One fancied how it would surge through the dim aisles of cathedral-like forests, ruffling the plumage of drowsy birds, stirring the surface of some dark pool, where the trout still slept, and making sibilant music among the drooping reeds.

The sky had now become delicately luminous, and a streak of saffron showed above the farthest roofs; a flock of little clouds huddled together above this, like timorous sheep at graze. The white star hung just above the cobbler's chimney, dangerously near, it seemed to us, who watched.

46

There were only two of us at the window now, for Angel had stolen away to explore every corner of the new environment, as was his custom. I could hear the soft opening and shutting of bureau drawers, and once, a grunting and straining, as of one engaged in severe manual labour.

A low whistle drew me to his side.

"What's up?" I demanded.

"Got this little old trunk open at last," he muttered, "full of women's junk. Funny stuff. Look."

Our heads touched as we bent curiously over the contents. It was a dingy and insignificant box on the outside, but it was lined with a gaily coloured paper, on which nosegays of spring flowers bent beneath the weight of silver butterflies, and sad-eyed cockatoos. The trays were full, as Angel had said, of women's things; delicate, ruffly frocks of pink and lilac; and undergarments edged with yellowing lace. A sweet scent rose from them, as of some gentle presence that strove to reach the light and air once more. A pair of little white kid slippers looked as though they longed to twinkle in and out beneath a soft silk skirt. Angel's mischievous brown hands dived among the light folds, discovering opera glasses,—(treasures to be secured if possible, against some future South Sea expedition), an inlaid box of old-fashioned trinkets, a coral necklace, gold-tasselled earrings, and a brooch of tortured locks of hair.

Angel's eyes were dancing above a gauze fan held coquettishly against his mouth of an impudent boy, but I gave no heed to him; I was busy with a velvet work-box that promised a solution of the mystery—for hidden away with thimble and scissors as one would secrete a treasure, was a fat little book, "The Mysteries of Udolpho." Some one had drawn on the fly leaf, very beautifully, I thought, a ribbed sea-shell, and on it had printed the words, "Lucy from Charles;" and on a scroll beneath the shell, in microscopic characters—"Bide the Time!"

My brother was looking over my shoulder now. We were filled with conjecture.

"Lucy," said Angel, "owned all this stuff, and Charles was her lover, of course. But who was she? Mrs. Handsomebody never had a daughter, I know, and if she had she'd never have allowed her to wear these things. Look how she jaws when Mary Ellen spends her wage on finery. I'll bet Lucy was a beauty. And she's dead too, you can bet, and Charles was her lover, and likely he's dead too. 'Bide the time,' eh? You see they're waitin' around yet—somewheres. Isn't it queer?"

The Seraph's voice came from the window in a sort of chant:

"The little white star has fallen down the cobbler's chimney!

"It has fallen down, and the cobbler is sewing it into a shoe!

"A milkman is wunning down the stweet!

"Tell you what," whispered Angel, "I'll show you what Lucy was like—just a little. I'll make a picture of her."

The space between two tall chests of drawers formed a sort of alcove in which stood a pier glass, whose tarnished frame was draped in white net. Before it Angel drew (without much caution) a high-backed chair, and on it he began his picture.

Over the seat and almost touching the floor, he draped a frilled petticoat, and against the back of the chair (with a foundation of formidable stays for support) he hung a garment, which, even then, he seemed to know for a camisole. Over all he laid a charming lilac silk gown, and under the hem in the most natural attitude peeped the little party slippers. A small lace and velvet bonnet with streamers was hung at the apex of the creation, and in her lap (for the time has come to use the feminine pronoun) he spread the gauzy fan. He hung over her tenderly, as an artist over his subject—each fold must be in place—the empty sleeves curved just so—one fancied a rounded chin beneath the velvet streamers, so artfully was it adjusted. Her reflection in the pier glass was superb!

"It is here!" chanted The Seraph. "Evwy bit of evwy fing is shinin'! Oh, Angel an' John, please look!"

We flew to the window and leaned across the sill.

It was a happy world that morning, glowing in the sweetest dawn that ever broke over roofs and chimney pots. The earth sang as she danced her dewy way among the paling stars. The little grey clouds blushed pink against the azure sky. Blossoming boughs of peach and apricot hung over the gates of heaven, and rosy spirals curled upward from two chimneys. Pink-footed pigeons strutted, rooketty-cooing along the roofs. They nodded their heads as though to affirm

48

the consummation of a miracle. "It is so—" they seemed to say—"It is indeed so—" One of them hopped upon the cobbler's chimney, peering earnestly into its depths. "It sees the star!" shouted The Seraph. "It sees the star and nods to it. 'I am higher now than you'— it says!"

Something—was it a breath? a sigh?—made me look back into the attic where Lucy's clothes clung to the high-backed chair, like flower petals blown against a wall. The pier-glass had caught all the glory of the morning and was releasing it in quivering spears of light that dazzled me for a moment; I rubbed my eyes, and stared, and shook a little, for in the midst of all this splendour I saw Lucy! No pallid, rigid ghost, but something warm, eager with life, spreading the folds of the lilac gown like a butterfly warming its new wings in the strength of the sun.

Her bosom rose and fell quickly, her eyes were fixed on me with a beseeching look, it seemed. I drew nearer—near enough to smell the faint perfume of her, and I saw then that she was not looking at me, but at the fat little book of "The Mysteries of Udolpho" which I still held in my hands. The book that Charles had given her! "Bide the time!" he had written, but she could bide the time no longer.

Proud as any knight before his lady, I strode forward, and pressed the book into her hands—saw her slender fingers curl around it— heard her little gasp of joy. I should not have been at all surprised had the door opened and Charles walked in.

As a matter of fact, the door did open and—Mrs. Handsomebody walked in.

IV

She gave a sort of gurgling cry, as though she were being strangled. Angel and The Seraph faced about to look at her in consternation, their hair wild in the wind, and the rising sun making an aureole about them. The four of us stared at each other in silence for a space, while the attic-room, with its cobwebs reeled—the sun rose, and sank, like a floundering ship, and Mrs. Handsomebody resembling, in my fancy, a hungry spider, in curl papers, considered which victim was ripest for slaughter.

49

"You—and you—and you—" she gobbled. "Oh, to think of it! No place safe! What you need is a strong man. We shall see! The very windows—burst from their bolts!" She slammed the casement and secured it, Angel and The Seraph darting from her path.

"Even a dead woman's clothes—to make a scarecrow of!" She pounced—I hid my face while she did it, but I heard a sinister rustling and the snap of a trunk lid. It was over. "Bide the time."

Ignominiously she herded us down the stairs; The Seraph making only one step at a time, led the way. Far down the drab vista of the back stairs that ended in the scullery, Mary Ellen's red, round face was seen for a moment, like a second rising sun, but vanished as suddenly as it had appeared, at a shout from Mrs. Handsomebody.

We were in the schoolroom now, placed before her in a row, as was her wont in times of retribution. Seated behind her desk she wore her purple dressing gown with magisterial dignity; the wart upon her chin quivered as she prepared to speak.

"Now, David," she said, rapping Angel smartly on the head, "can you say anything in explanation of this outrage upon my property? Hold your head up and toe out, please."

Angel looked at his hands. "Nuffin' to explain," he said sulkily. "Just went an' did it."

"Oh I thought so," said our governess. "It was just one of these seemingly irresistible impulses that have so often proved disastrous for all concerned. If your father knew—" she bit off the words as though they had a pleasant, if acrid taste—"if your poor father knew of your criminal proclivities, he would be a crushed man. A crushed man."

The Seraph was staring at her chin.

Then—"I have one too," he said gently.

"One what?" Her tone should have warned him. "One wart," he went on, with easy modesty. "It's just a little one. It can't wiggle—like yours—but it's gwowing nicely. Would you care to see it?"

Mrs. Handsomebody affected not to hear him. She stared sombrely at Angel and me, but I believe The Seraph sealed our fate, for, after a moment's deliberation, she said curtly; "I shall have to beat you for this."

She gave us six apiece, and I could not help noticing that, though The Seraph was the youngest and tenderest, his six were the most stinging.

When we had been sent to our bedroom to say our prayers, and change our pitifully inadequate night clothes for day things, I put the question that was burning in my mind.

"Did either of you see her?"

"Who?"

"Lucy, sitting there in the chair."

Angel's brown eyes were blank.

"I saw her clothes. What sickens me is that the dragon took that spy-glass. You see if I don't get it yet." (Mrs. Handsomebody was "the dragon" in our vernacular.)

"Did you see her, Seraph?"

The Seraph was sitting on the floor, his head on his knees. He raised a tear-flushed face.

"I'm 'most too cwushed to wemember," he said, huskily. "But I fink Lucy was fat. It's a vewy bad fing to be fat, 'cos the cane hurts worser."

I turned from such infantile imbecility to the exhilarating reflection that I was the only one to whom Lucy had shown herself—her chosen knight!

I was burning to do her service, yet the passage that led to the attic stronghold was well guarded. Two days had passed before I made the attempt. I had been sent upstairs from the tea-table to wash my hands—though they were only comfortably soiled—and after I had dipped them in a basin of water that had done service for both Angel and The Seraph, I gave them a good rub on my trouser legs, as I tip-toed to the foot of the attic stairs. Cautiously, with fast-beating heart, I mounted, and tried the door. It was locked fast. I pressed my eye against the keyhole, and made out in the gloom the dark shape of the trunk, sinister, forbidding, inaccessible. No rustle of lilac silk, no faintest perfume, no appealing sigh from the gentle Lucy greeted me. All was dark and quiet. "Bide the time!" Who knew but that some day I might set her free?

51

Yet my throat ached as I slowly made my way back to the table, presented my hands for a rather sceptical inspection by Mrs. Handsomebody, and dropped languidly into my seat.

The Seraph gave me a look of sympathy—even understanding—perhaps he had heard me mount the distant attic stairs; his hearing was wonderfully acute. He chewed in silence for a moment and then he made one of those seemingly irrelevant remarks of his that, somehow, always set our little world a-rocking.

"One fing about Lucy," he said, "she was always sweet-tempud."

"Who?" snapped Mrs. Handsomebody.

"Lucy—" repeated The Seraph. "Such a sweet-tempud gell."

Mrs. Handsomebody leaned over him, and gobbled and threatened. The Seraph preserved a remarkable calm, considering that he was the storm centre. He even raised his small forefinger before his face and looked at it thoughtfully. His speculative gaze travelled from it to Mrs. Handsomebody's chin. I perceived then that he was comparing warts!

Chapter IV

A Merry Interlude

I

My brothers and I were hanging over the gate that barred our way to the outer world, and singing, as loudly as we could, considering the pressure of the top bar on our young stomachs. We sang to keep warm, for Mrs. Handsomebody had decreed that no reefers were to be worn till the first of December. So, though November was raw, she maintained her discipline and refused to mollycoddle us.

It was the fifth, and Angel chanted in that flute-like treble of his, that made passersby turn and smile at him:

> *"Remember, remember the fifth of November,*
> *Gunpowder, treason and plot—"*

Then The Seraph added his little pipe:

> *"I see no weason why gunpowder tweason*
> *Should ever be forgot."*

Then we shouted it all together.

Our neighbour, Mr. Mortimer Pegg, who had never forgiven us for our share in the treasure hunt, came out of his house at that moment, and drew up before us.

"This noise, you know," he said, in his precise way, "is affecting my wife's health deleteriously. She has gone to bed with a migraine."

"Why don't you put him out," suggested The Seraph.

Mr. Pegg eyed him severely, yet I thought I perceived a twinkle in his eye.

"It's Guy Fawkes day," I explained. "You see, it must never be forgot."

"It is a mistake in these enlightened days to keep up such old animosities," replied our neighbour. "For all you know I might be

53

his direct descendant. If you must celebrate his undoing, better take these three sixpences and make yourselves ill on lemon fizz, or pink marshmallows, or vile licorice cigars."

He placed a coin in each outstretched hand, and, without waiting for thanks, strode briskly down the street. We gazed after him, knocked speechless by this great beaker of bounty that had rolled in upon the flat expanse of our afternoon. Mr. Pegg, in his shiny top hat and neat Prince Albert moved away in the ruddy November sunlight as in a halo of opulence. Never before had we appreciated the princely turn of his toes beneath their drab spats, the flash of his twirled walking-stick. We resolved to keep him in mind. He was a neighbour worth having. Angel even suggested certain time-honoured ditties of boyhood, which, shouted in chorus, would be almost certain to have a disastrous effect on a female addicted to migraine.

A deputation, consisting of The Seraph, then waited on Mrs. Handsomebody, to explain that our neighbour, Mr. Pegg, having been charmed by our singing, had presented us each with a sixpence, with the earnest injunction that the coin be expended on currant buns at the grocer's. The Seraph came back triumphant with the necessary consent.

"We can go," he said, "but we're not to take a bite till we're back home. It's suppwising she'd let us do it."

"Not a bit," said Angel cynically, "she knows they'll spoil our appetite for tea."

The grocer was a fierce, red-bearded man who kept his wife in a little wooden stall, where she took in the constant flow of wealth extorted from his customers.

We had told The Seraph that she was thus confined by her gloomy spouse, in order that she might be fattened for slaughter, and his eyes were large with pity as he stood on tiptoe to hand our three sixpences through the little wicket. The grocer's wife leaned forward to look at him, her plump underlip, after two futile attempts to form a chin, subsiding into a large white neck.

The Seraph's look of pity deepened to horror. "You must be almost weady," he gasped.

"Ready? Ready for what, my little love?"

"Stickin'—oo, will it hurt vewy much?"

"Bless the child. What does he mean?"

"He's not very well," I explained. "I think he's delirious."

"That's why we brought him here to get a cool drink," added Angel, hurriedly, and between us we led the recreant to the little table in the rear of the shop where the grocer had set out three glasses of ginger beer and a plate of mixed cakes. Five minutes of unalloyed bliss followed and we were just draining off the last dregs and cleaning up the crumbs, when a bullet-headed boy stuck his head in at the door.

"Dorg's 'ere again," he said, laconically. "Nosin' abaht in the gabbage 'eap."

"Tie a can on 'is tile," said the grocer.

The boy disappeared, and the three of us pushed back our chairs and followed in his wake, scenting adventure in the littered yard behind the shop with its strange odours of bygone fruit and greens.

The dog, a small, black, Scottish terrier, was dragging an end of Boulogna sausage from the garbage heap. The bullet-headed boy winked at us, selected an empty can from the heap, produced a piece of string from his pocket, and grasped the terrier by the collar. But only for a moment. With a rush of concentrated fury it flew at his legs, gave him a sharp snap, and darted back to its sausage, with a warning glean of its eyes in our direction.

"Ow," yelled the boy, doubling up, "'e's bit me sumpfin' cruel! You see if I daon't brain 'im for that!"

He snatched up an axe and brandished it. The terrier dropped its sausage and showed its little pointed teeth.

We three, with one impulse, flung ourselves between it and the boy.

"You dare touch that dog," shouted Angel.

"Oo's goin' to stop me, Mister Nosey Parker?" sneered the boy, with a flourish of his axe.

"I am," said Angel, "'cos it's my dog, see?" He coolly turned his back

55

on the boy and bent over the terrier, who came to him cautiously, sniffing his legs.

"Your dorg!" scoffed the boy, "w'y daon't yer feed 'im then? 'E's arf starved, 'e is. Yer ought to be 'ad up fer perwention of cruelty to hanimals. It's a disgrice."

"We've only owned him a little while," explained Angel, "and he strayed away. He'll be jolly glad to get home again—won't you, Rover? Give us that bit of string and I'll lead him."

The boy, suddenly friendly, in one of those swiftly changing moods of boyhood, assisted in the tying of the string to the little dog's collar, though he cast a longing look at its stout fringed tail that was so admirably built to further the riotous bouncings of an empty tin can.

We led him triumphantly through the shop into the street, and we trotted in silence for a space, staring in rapt admiration of the little black paws that padded along in such a business-like fashion beside us, the knowingly-pointed ears, and valiant tail carried at a jaunty angle above the sturdy hind-quarters.

When we reached our own quiet street we stopped. The Seraph looked in the bag of buns.

"May I give him mine?" he asked.

"Good boy," said Angel, and The Seraph presented the little dog with the large currant bun. We were charmed indeed when he sat up for it in the most approved trained-animal posture, with short fore-legs crossed on his plump hairy breast. How often had we longed for the joyous companionship of our old four-footed friends, the comfort of a soft warm tongue on one's cheek, the sensitive muzzle pressed into one's palm, the look of loving confidence in the deep brown eyes.

But our governess hated dogs, and we were expressly forbidden to so much as pat the head of any stray canine that thrust an inquiring nose between the bars of her gate. Therefore, it was with sad foreboding that we watched the bun disappear. The Scotty held it between his forepaws and bit off decent mouthfuls, without sign of greed or haste. By his bearing and by his shining silver collar we knew that he was, or had been some one's cherished pet.

56

The bun had cheered him wonderfully, for, as we moved homeward, he leaped playfully at his leash, and catching it in his teeth, worried it in an abandon of glee.

We made no plans. We had no hopes. We merely were drawn by habit and necessity to the place where, we knew, desperate trouble awaited us. At the gate we halted.

"We might take him into the yard to play for a little while," I said. "P'raps we could carry him upstairs wrapped in my coat, and hide him under the bed. Maybe he'd get so awful good he'd live under the bed, and we could save our food for him, and get up nights to play with him."

As if to show his appreciation of the plan, the Scotty raised himself on his hind quarters, paddling the air with his forepaws in excited appeal, and giving vent to sharp, staccato barks.

The next instant the front door was thrown open, and Mary Ellen, her cap askew, dashed down the steps to meet us.

"Wheriver have ye been so long?" she ejaculated. "An' have ye been tould the news? 'Tis hersilf has taken a tumble, an' put her knee out so the doctor says. I'd jist been clanin' up the panthry shelves, an' she got up on a chair to see whether I'd maybe missed the top one, an' I must have left a knob of soap on the chair, for the next thing I knew she was stretched on the flure, an' I had to fetch the doctor, an' he says she'll have to kape to her room for a fortnight or more, an' the lord only knows how I'm to wait on her an' manage the three av ye, wid yer pranks an' all!"

The Seraph turned a somersault; then I turned a somersault; then Angel turned two; then the Scotty sat up, paddled the air with his forepaws, and sneezed twice.

Mary Ellen was genuinely shocked.

"I do belave," she said, solemnly, "that you've stones in your breasts instid av hearts—but you're jist like all men folk—if they think there's a good time in sthore for them, the women can suffer all they like, more shame to them." She was so worked up that she did not notice that the little dog had followed us into the house, until he was sitting up in the kitchen, his forepaws paddling the air, his tail thudding on the floor. Then she said, brimming over with admiration, though she tried to look severe;

57

"And if you think I'll have sthray dawgs in my kitchen you're very much mistook.... Aw, it's a darlin' wee thing, isn't it?" For the Scotty, seeing that she had seated herself, had jumped to her lap and now sat there, nose in air, looking superbly at home.

We closed about her, telling, in chorus, the story of the bullet-headed boy, and the garbage heap, and enlarging dramatically on the episode of the tin can.

"And may we please keep him?" we entreated, "just for a few days till we find the owner of it! Mrs. Handsomebody will never know, for he can live in the coal cellar 'cept when we take him little walks on a string!"

"If you don't let me do this I'll never marry you, so there!" This from Angel.

"Have it your own way, thin," moaned Mary Ellen, capitulating, as usual, under the fire of Angel's pleading, "but moind, if she iver finds us out, it's mesilf will be walkin' the streets widout a character."

II

So began a merry interlude in the drabness of the Handsomebody regime. Mrs. Handsomebody kept to her room for nearly three weeks, unable to put her foot to the floor. On the first evening, she called us to her bedside; and, while we stood in a row, bewildered before the phenomenon of seeing her prostrate, she lectured us solemnly on the duties and responsibilities of our position, and implored us not to make the period of her enforced retirement a nightmare, because of our pranks. We promised, marvelling that bed-clothes could be kept so tidy, and fervently wishing she would display the knee that had been so severely "put out." It was a commonplace for Mrs. Handsomebody's temper to be thus afflicted, but her knee, never.

When we returned to the kitchen, we found Mary Ellen sitting in a pensive attitude. Her forefinger pressed against her knit brow, her stout ankles crossed.

"The little dawg has been tellin' me a secret," she volunteered in explanation, "a deep, dark secret. She's been tellin' me in a way of spakin' that she's a lady-dawg, God help her."

"But how did she tell you, Mary Ellen? Did she speak out loud?" We were breathless with excitement.

"She did not. I ast her, for I had me suspicion, if she was a lady-dawg an' I sez—'If yez are wag yer tail three times,' an' the words was scarce off me tongue, whin she wagged her tail three times."

It was a marvel. Oh, these were going to be great days!

"If you're a lady-dog, wag your tail three times," I ordered, squatting to peer into the sagacious brown eyes.

Three times the stocky tail thumped the floor.

Then Angel put the question, and was answered with equal promptitude.

It was The Seraph's turn. With an insinuating smile he said: "If you are a gennelman dog wag your tail fwee times."

But before there was time for so much as one wag, Mary Ellen caught the too-eager tail in a restraining grasp.

"Now have done wid your nonsinse," she commanded. "Ye'll have the pore crature that worried it'll set up barkin', an' if the misthress did know, there be's a dawg in the house, she'd likely just throw a fit an' die."

"Is it a vewy barkable dog?" queried The Seraph.

"All dogs is barkable," said Mary Ellen, "and what we'll have to do is to kape her as quate as possible and pray that her owner'll come along this way, for turn her out I will not. It's easy seein' she's a pet be the ways of her."

"It says 'Giftie' on her collar," Angel announced, separating the short, shaggy coat to read. "That must be her name. Hello, Giftie! Sit up, Giftie!"

So Giftie she was, and, for a long three weeks, our joy and our delight.

Was ever little body so full of spirit and the pride of life? The

59

kitchen became her own domain where the three of us fought for the position of her most abject slave. Even Mary Ellen could scarcely work for watching her antics with an old stocking, which she pretended was a rat. Once she caught a live mouse and set us all shouting. Mary Ellen, in her excitement, upset a gravy-boat of hot gravy, and The Seraph slipped and sat down in it, and Giftie gambolling, mouse in mouth, ran through it and tracked it over the freshly scrubbed boards. If she had been a tigress with her prey she could not have been more ferocious with the mouse. She snarled at it: she worried it: she threw it up in the air and caught it: she laid it on the scullery floor and rolled on it: and when, finally, it ceased to squirm beneath her, she lay quite still, gazing pensively up at us with liquid eyes, and only now and then twitching her hind-quarters to remind her victim that she was still on the job.

One never-to-be-forgotten day she rollicked into the kitchen proudly carrying Mrs. Handsomebody's solemn black shoe, which had been standing with its mate beneath Mrs. Handsomebody's bed. Before our horrified eyes, she worried it till the shoe-laces cracked about her head; threw it up and caught it, as she had the mouse; then taking it to her own bed in the scullery, she laid it there and rolled on it.

When Mary Ellen had wrested the shoe from Giftie, she crept upstairs, her heart in her mouth, and restored it to its place beneath the bed.

"It was a marvel," she said afterwards, "how the scallywag did what she did widout wakenin' her, for there was the mistress sleepin' on the broad of her back, and her two shoes, and her bed-socks scattered over the flure, and the pot of cold crame knocked off the chair at the head of her bed, and the half of it et. It's mesilf will dance for joy whin that little tormint gets took away."

Inquiries were made of all the errand boys, but not one had heard of a lost dog. We came to dread the sound of the door-bell lest it should herald some determined grown-up come to snatch our treasure from us. Mr. Watlin, the butcher's young man, and Mary Ellen's favoured "follower" of the moment, took a lively interest in the affair. He was of the opinion that if Mrs. Handsomebody once saw the dog nothing would induce her to send it away. And he brought offerings of raw meat in his pocket to make her plump and glossy. Giftie grew plumper and glossier every day.

Then, when two weeks had passed, she achieved the crowning

triumph of her stay with us. It was a heavy morning of dense November fog, and the gas was still burning in the dining-room when we came down to breakfast. Mary Ellen did not bring us our porridge, as usual, neither did Giftie run in to greet us; so, after a moment's impatient wriggling in our chairs, we went to the kitchen to investigate. Giftie was nowhere in sight. Mary Ellen sat in an attitude of complete abandon, by the dresser, her apron over her head, her arms hanging loosely at her sides. Was Giftie dead? Had her owner come to fetch her? What horror had overcast the sun? We deluged her with questions, pulling the apron off her head, and dragging her from the chair.

"Och, it's a terror she is," Mary Ellen said, at last. "Come wid me to the scullery an' ye'll see what she's got in the bed wid her."

There was not much light in the scullery so we could not at first distinguish what lay on the mat beside Giftie. It moved; it snuffled; no—they moved; they snuffled. There were three of them. All at once it burst upon us that they were puppies—her puppies—our puppies—one apiece! We flopped on the floor beside her. She darted from her bed—licked our hands—snapped at our ankles—ran back to them—and, finally tremulous with excitement, allowed us to take them in our arms (The Seraph wrapped his in the skirt of his fresh holland smock) and sit blissfully in a row.

We stroked the soft licked fur of their glossy coats; we examined their tiny sharp black nails; their blindness only endeared them the more to us.

There we were found by Mr. Watlin.

"'Ere's a picnic," he said. "'Ere's a bloomin' picnic." He caught up the nearest puppy, and turned it over in an experienced hand. "Tiles must be cut," he added.

"Tails cut! Oh, no," I expostulated, "Giftie's tail isn't cut. Please don't."

"All terriers should 'ave their tiles cut," said Mr. Watlin, firmly. "If the mother dog's tile isn't cut, is that any reason w'y 'er hoffspring should be disfigured in a like manner? Now's the time."

"But it'll hurt," pleaded The Seraph. Do you do it wif a knife?"

"I bites 'em orf," replied Mr. Watlin, laconically, "an' it don't 'urt a bit."

61

"In this world," he went on, "a lot depends on the way you does a thing. F'rinstance, when I kill a lamb or a steer, do I kill 'im brutally? Not at all. I runs 'im up an' down the slaughter yard to get 'is circulation up—I strokes 'im on the neck, an' tells 'im wot a fine feller 'e is, till 'e's in such good spirits that 'e' tikes the killin' as a joke. Just a part of the gime, as it were. Sime with these 'ere pups. They'd like 'aving their tiles bit orf by me."

We looked at the puppies doubtfully. It was hard to believe that they would really like it, and we were relieved when Mary Ellen broke in—

"They will not be cut, nor bit, nor interfered wid in anny way. If Giftie's owner likes a long tail on her, he'd want a long tail on her puppies wouldn't he? That stands to reason, Mr. Watlin, don't it? and the owner may walk in here anny day."

How we hated that nebulous owner! And now another cloud loomed on our horizon. Mrs. Handsomebody was getting better. She had sat up on a chair by the bedside; she had, with Mary Ellen's help, walked across the room; she had, all alone, walked down the hallway; she had come to the head of the stairs. She was like the man in the ghost story, who, fresh from his grave, called to his wife—snugly sleeping above—"Mary, I'm at the foot of the stairs.... Mary, I'm half way up." We, too, shuddered in anticipation. And Mary Ellen was almost as nervous as we, for hers was the responsibility.

The puppies were more entrancing every day. Tiny slips of dewy blue showed between their furry eyelids. They learned to walk, and roll over, and to right themselves after being turned over by their mother's playful paws. We were squatting on the floor very busy with them, when Mary Ellen entered, round-eyed with fear.

"'Tis herself is in the dining-room," she gasped.

"Not Mrs. Handsomebody?"

"Sorra a thing else. Put them pups in their basket and come out and shut the dure. Ye'd better go into the yard and be at some quate game. Oh, Lord—" and she hurried back to her mistress.

This time we were safe, but there was tomorrow ahead, with certain discovery.

Mr. Watlin, propped in the open doorway, brought his ingenious mind to bear upon the problem.

"Now if Mrs. 'Andsomebody could be put under an obligation to that little dog, she'd probably tike it right into 'er 'eart and 'ome. If that little dog, f'rinstance, should save Mrs. 'Andsomebody from drowning—does she ever go in bathing?"

"Likely, at her age, in December!" sneered Mary Ellen. "Try again."

"We might hold her under water in the bath-tub till Giftie would fish her out," suggested Angel.

It was a colourful spectacle to visualize, and we dallied with it a space before abandoning it as impracticable. It seemed too much to hope that Mrs. Handsomebody, the bath-tub and Giftie could all be assembled at the critical moment.

But Mr. Watlin was not to be rebuffed. "Then there's burglars," he went on. "Suppose Mrs. 'Andsomebody's valuables was to be rescued from a burglar for 'er. She wouldn't be able to do enough for a little dog that 'ad chased 'im out of this very scullery, f'rinstance."

We were thrilled by hope. "But where is the burglar?"

"Well, I could produce the burglar in a pinch. He's reformed but he'd undertake a little job like this if he know'd it was for partic'lar friends of mine, and not a bit of 'arm in it. Is it a go?"

Mystery brooded over the house of Handsomebody all that afternoon and evening. We were allowed to have no finger in this portentous pie.

Mr. Watlin, with some small assistance from Mary Ellen, engineered the thing himself. We were sent to bed at the usual hour, and played at burglars on, and under, the bed, to while away the intervening hours.

III

It must have been almost midnight when our hearts were made to beat in our throats by such an uproar in the scullery, as seemed to cleave the darkness like a thunderbolt. Giftie appeared to be choking in her effort to unloose, all at once, a torrent of ferocious barks. A window shook, glass broke, a shutter slammed. Then followed a moment of awful silence before she settled down to a methodical yapping. We heard Mary Ellen run down the back stairs.

We clambered out of bed, and tumbled into the hall. Mrs. Handsomebody was there before us, a gigantic shadow of her thrown on the walls by a candle she held unsteadily in her hand.

"Merciful Heaven!" she was saying under her breath. "What can have happened!" She motioned us to fall in behind her, and it was plain that, crippled as she was, she intended to interpose her body, in its flannel nightgown, between us and whatever danger lurked below. She made the descent clinging to the bannister, the three of us jostling each other in the rear, and, once, nearly precipitated on her back by a caper of Angel's on the edge of a step.

Mary Ellen met us in the dining-room, her face pale with excitement.

"It was a burglar in the scullery, ma'am," she burst out, never looking at us. "It's a mercy we wasn't all murthered in our beds this night—the windy's broke, an' the shutter's pried loose, and a bag full av all the things off the sideboard is settin' on the flure. Sure, I heard the steps av him runnin' full lick down the lane—"

Mrs. Handsomebody looked at her bereft sideboard, and dropped into a chair with a gasp.

"Are you sure he's gone?"

"Yes'm. I stuck me head out the windy and seen him."

"You're a brave girl. Get me the bitters. Yes, and lock the door into the scullery—stay, what dog was it that barked?"

Mary Ellen hung her head. "The dawg the little boys have been keepin' this bit while. It does no harm at all."

Mrs. Handsomebody's face was a mask. She said composedly: "Well, get the bitters and then bring in the dog."

Mary Ellen did as she was bid.

Enter now Giftie, tail up, ears pricked, the picture of conscious well-doing. She went straight to Mrs. Handsomebody, sniffed her ankles; wagged her tail in appreciation of the odour of the liniment that emanated from the injured lady; and finally sat up before her with an ingratiating paddling of the forepaws.

Mrs. Handsomebody regarded her sombrely. "May I ask how long you have harboured this stray?"

"Just since the day ye fell, ma'am, and I was that upset that I was scarce in me right moind, and indade, it's hersilf has saved us from robbery and mebbe murther this night wid her barkin'."

Giftie, tired of sitting up without reward or encouragement, had trotted quietly out of the room. She now came back waddling with importance, a pup in her mouth. She laid it at the feet of our governess as though to say—"There now, what do you make of that?"

"Horrors!" cried Mrs. Handsomebody, drawing back, as though the puppy were a serpent.

With a joyful kick of the heels, Giftie was off again. In breathless silence we waited. The second puppy, sleepy and squirming, was laid beside its brother.

"I presume you have another?" said Mrs. Handsomebody in a controlled voice but gripping the arms of her chair.

Giftie brought the other.

"Oh, Mrs. Handsomebody!" I implored, "please, please, let us keep them! They're as good as gold, and they'd guard the house and everything—and maybe save you from drowning some time. Don't take them from us, pl-ease!" The Seraph, in sympathy, began to cry. Angel picked up his pup and held it against his breast.

"Silence!" rapped out Mrs. Handsomebody. "Mary Ellen, fetch The Times. And just look in the scullery to see that all is quiet there. Fetch the bag left by the robber."

Mrs. Handsomebody sipped her bitters while Mary Ellen did her behests. Each of us cuddled his own puppy, and Giftie began an energetic search for a flea.

Had our hearts not been in the grip of apprehension we should have laughed at the figure cut by Mary Ellen, panting under the sack of

65

plate. Mr. Watlin's burglar had done his job well, and Mrs. Handsomebody groaned when she saw her most cherished possessions tumbled in such a reckless fashion. But not a thing was missing, and when they had been replaced on the sideboard, she turned briskly to The Times. She ran a long white finger down the Lost column.

"Ah, here we are—" she announced, complacently—"Pay attention, boys," and she read:

> "Reward for information leading to the recovery of Scottish terrier, female, wearing silver collar engraved, Giftie, stolen or strayed from 5 Argyle Road, on November third. Anyone detaining after this notice will be prosecuted."

"You see," exclaimed Mrs. Handsomebody, triumphantly, "you have made yourselves liable to a heavy fine, or even imprisonment, by detaining what is, I presume, a very valuable beast. Argyle Road—a very good locality—is not too great a distance for you to walk. In the morning, we shall return that dog and her—er—young, and I see nothing amiss in your accepting a suitable reward. Not a word now! No insubordination, mind. I won't have it. David, John, Alexander, listen—I am in no mood to be trifled with. Put down those squirming creatures and march to your bed!"

Giftie's hour had struck. It was no use rebelling. With bitter composure, we carried our beloved to the scullery, and laid them on the mat beside their mother. It was not until we were safe in bed that our pent up fury broke loose; and we pounded the pillows, and cursed the name of womankind.

Women! Tyrants! Mischievous busybodies!

"When I'm a man," said Angel, suddenly, "I'll marry a woman, and I'll beat her every day."

"Me too!" cried The Seraph, stoutly, "I'll mawy two—fat ones—an' beat 'em bofe."

For myself, I was inclined for an unhampered bachelorhood, but it soothed my wounded spirit to picture these three hapless females in the grip of Angel and The Seraph, and the music of their outcries lulled me fast asleep.

IV

We found next morning that Mrs. Handsomebody and Mary Ellen had never gone back to bed all night, but had kept watch in the dining-room till daylight, when Mary Ellen had been dispatched to find a policeman. He was in the kitchen now, a commanding figure, making notes in a little book; and seeming to derive great benefit from his conversation with Mary Ellen.

A new arrival was a wheeled-chair to convey Mrs. Handsomebody to 5 Argyle Road. Therefore, about ten o'clock, after the most exhausting preparations, we set out, a singular party; Mrs. Handsomebody enthroned in the chair, mistress of herself (and every one else) her black-gloved hands crossed on her lap; Mary Ellen, hot, straining over the wheeled-chair, lest her mistress get an unseemly bump at the crossing; Angel and I, bearing between us a covered hamper containing the three pups; while Giftie and The Seraph in the abandon of youth and ignorance, sported on the outskirts of the group.

The way was long, and our arms ached with the weight of the hamper, when we stopped before the gate of Number 5 Argyle Road. It was an imposing house in its own grounds; large clipped trees stood about; and a bent old gardener was doing something to one of those, while a tall grey-haired woman in mannish tweeds superintended the work. A Scottish terrier, fit mate for Giftie, was digging furiously at the root of the tree. He discovered our presence first, and, before we had time to introduce ourselves, he and Giftie, with bristling backs, were jumping about one another in a sort of friendly hostility, and filling the air with barks of greeting. Giftie, then, darted for the hamper, sniffed it, ran back to the other Scotty, and bit him so that he yelped. All was confusion.

The tall lady came toward us smiling broadly. She exclaimed above the din: "How can I thank you? I see you have brought home our little wanderer—Giftie, how can you treat Colin so? Poor Colin—lift him up, Giles, she's going to bite him again—I suppose there are pups in the hamper. Let's see, boys."

We uncovered the hamper proudly. The three puppies lay curled like little sea anemones. Giftie tried to get in the hamper with them, but her mistress restrained her gently, while she lifted them out, one by one, and examined each, critically, Mrs. Handsomebody watching her all the while with an expression of disapproval, that bordered on disgust.

67

The tall lady, quite oblivious to all this, seated herself on the ground with the puppies on her lap, muttering ecstatically-"Perfect beauties—what luck! Giftie, you're a wonder!" Whereupon Giftie tried to kiss her on the ear. The bent old gardener, brought Colin to us and made him shake hands, and we thought him very long-faced and dour after roguish Giftie.

Presently Mrs. Handsomebody spoke in her most decisive tones:

"I fear I shall take a chill if I remain in this damp place. Come boys. Mary Ellen, kindly reverse the chair!"

The tall lady rose to her feet.

"Oh, please, come in and have something hot, and tell me all about it. And there's the reward."

"I thank you," replied Mrs. Handsomebody, "I shall not venture to leave my chair. As for the dog, it came to us several weeks ago, when I was ill; hence the delay in returning it—and its young."

"Your grandchildren?" questioned the tall lady abruptly.

"My pupils, and, for the present, my wards," replied Mrs. Handsomebody frigidly.

"Wish I could steal them," said the lady. "If I'd dogs and boys too, I'd be happy. These are darlings." She turned to us then. "Boys, do you like Giftie very much?"

"Oh, we love her," we chorused.

"Would you like one of her puppies for your very own to keep?"

Would we? We couldn't speak for longing.

Mrs. Handsomebody spoke for us.

"I allow no pets, canine or otherwise."

The tall lady scowled. "But these are valuable dogs."

"All dogs are alike to me. Canines."

The tall lady gave something between a snort and a sigh.

"Would you allow them to accept a sovereign apiece then?"

"That would be permissible."

"I shall be back directly," and with astonishing speed she ran to the house with Colin and Giftie barking on either side of her. It was but a moment till she returned and pressed a golden sovereign into each languid hand. The sight of so much bullion all at once braced us for the moment, and we forgot to be miserable. She came with us to the gate, asking a dozen questions about ourselves, and our father, and Giftie's stay with us. Giftie had to be restrained from following us, and with sinking hearts we kissed her little black nose and said good-bye.

"Good-bye!" called the tall lady, "come again any time! Come and spend the day with us!"

Our governess called us peremptorily. She was half a block in advance.

When we reached the chair, she said, in a conciliatory tone: "I shall arrange for you to have some unusual treat from your reward, some concerts and lantern lectures suited to your years, and maybe, as the Christmas Season approaches, even a pantomime. What do you say?"

I looked at the woman. Was she mad to imagine that such paltry, sickly treats could make up for the loss of three pups whose eyes were beginning to open? My own eyes smarted with tears. I looked at Mary Ellen. Two bright drops hung on her cheeks as she laboured behind the chair. I looked at Angel. He was balancing himself on the curb with an air of desperate indifference. I could hear The Seraph weeping as he brought up the rear.

I lingered behind to offer him a suck of a piece of licorice I had. Then I saw that he had stopped and was hunched above the grating of a sewer. I could but think that his spirits had reached such an ebb that nothing save the contemplation of the foulest depths might salve his misery. But I was mistaken! His hand moved above the grating. Something flashed. Then I swelled my chest with pride in him. Truly, The Seraph was a brother to be proud of—a fellow of sturdy passions, not to be trifled with!

He had chucked his sovereign down the sewer!

Chapter V

Freedom

I

Life became dull indeed after Giftie was taken from us. November drew on to December; beating rains kept us indoors for days at a time. Mrs. Handsomebody had a horror of wet feet. With faces pressed against streaming window panes, we watched for the blurred progress of the lamplighter down the street, as the one excitement of the day. Even our friend the Bishop deserted us and went for a long stay in the south of France. Angel developed a sore throat just before Christmas so we had no part in the Christmas music in the Cathedral. The toy pistols sent by our father did not arrive till a fortnight after Christmas, and when they did arrive, the joy of possessing them was short-lived, for after Angel had cracked a pane of glass with his, and I had hit Mary Ellen on the ear, so that it was swollen and red for days, Mrs. Handsomebody confiscated them all as dangerous weapons to be kept till we were beyond her control.

She gave us each a new prayer book illustrated by pictures from the Gospel. I coloured the pictures in mine with crayons, and got my hands rulered for it; Angel traded his with one of the choir boys for a catapult which he successfully kept in concealment, with occasional forays on back alley cats. The Seraph was immensely pleased with his. He carried it about in his blouse, producing it, now and again, for reference, with pretended solemnity. His manner became unbearably clerical. I think he felt himself, at least, a Canon.

The winter wore on, and we became pale and peevish from lack of air, when all our little world was quickened by the coming of the telegram.

It had come while we were at lessons. Angel and I were standing before our governess with our hands behind our backs, when Mary Ellen burst in at the door. I had been stumbling over the names of the Channel Islands, and I stopped with my mouth open, relieved to see Mrs. Handsomebody's look of indignation raised from my face to that of Mary Ellen.

"Is that the way I have instructed you to enter the room where I sit?" asked Mrs. Handsomebody sternly.

"Lord, no, ma'am," gasped Mary Ellen, "but it's a telegram I've brung for ye, an' I thought as it was likely bad news, ye wouldn't want to be kept waitin' while I'd rap at the dure!" She presented the bit of paper between a wet thumb and forefinger.

"You may take your seats," said Mrs. Handsomebody coldly, to us.

Angel and I slipped into our places at the long book-littered table, on either side of The Seraph. We were thus placed, in order that his small plump person should prove an obstacle to familiar intercourse between Angel and myself during school hours; and, as our intercourse usually took the form of punches in the short ribs, or wet paper pellets aimed at an unoffending nose, The Seraph was frequently the recipient of such pleasantries. He bore them with good humour and stoicism.

"I'll bet anything," whispered Angel, over The Seraph's curls, "that it's a telegram from father saying that he's coming to fetch us! Wouldn't that be jolly? And she's waxy about it too—see how white she's gone!"

Mrs. Handsomebody rose.

"Boys," she said, in her most frigid manner, "owing to news of a sudden bereavement, I shall not be able to continue your lessons today—nor tomorrow. You will, I hope, make the most of the time intervening. You were in a shocking state of unpreparedness both in History and Geography this morning. Keep your little brother out of mischief, and remember," raising her long forefinger, "you are not, under any consideration, to leave the premises during my absence. As I have a great responsibility on your account, I wish to be certain that you are not endangering yourselves in the street. When I return we shall undertake some long walks."

Picking up the telegram from the floor where it had fallen, Mrs. Handsomebody slowly left the room, and closed the door behind her.

"She's always jawing about her responsibility," muttered Angel resentfully. "Why don't she let us run about like other boys 'stead of mewing us up like a parcel of girls? I'll be shot if I stand it!"

71

"What are the Channel Islands anyhow?" I asked to change the subject. "I'd just got to Jersey, Guernsey, when I got stuck."

"Jersey, Guernsey, Sweater, Sock and Darn," replied my elder, emphasizing the last named.

"Was the telegram from father?" interrupted The Seraph. "Is he comin' home?"

"No, silly," replied Angel. "Some one belonging to Mrs. Handsomebody is dead. She's goin' to the funeral, I s'pose. Whoever can it be, John? Didn't know she had any people."

"A whole day away," I mused, "it has never happened before."

I looked at Angel, and Angel looked at me—such looks as might be exchanged by lion cubs in captivity. We remembered our old home with its stretch of green lawn, the dogs, the stable with the sharp sweet smell of hay, and the pigeons, sliding and "rooketty-cooing" on the roof. Here, the windows of our schoolroom looked out on a planked back yard, and our daily walks with Mrs. Handsomebody were dreary outings indeed.

Of a sudden Angel threw his Geography into the air. His brown eyes were sparkling.

"We'll make a day of it, Lieutenant," he cried, slapping me on the shoulder. He always called me Lieutenant where mischief was a-foot. "Such a day as never was! We'll do every blessed thing we're s'posed not to! Most of all—we'll run the streets!"

At that instant, Mary Ellen opened the door and put her rosy face in.

"She do be packin' her bag, byes," she whispered, "she's takin' the eliven o'clock train, an' she won't be back till tomorrow at noon. Now what d'ye think o' that? She's awful quate, but she's niver spilt a tear fer him that I could spot."

"For who?"

"Why, her brother to be sure. It's him that's dead. It's a attack of brownkitis that's carried him off so suddint. Her only brother an'— yes, ma'am, I'm comin'," her broad face disappeared, "I was on'y tellin' the young gintlemen to be nice an' quate while I git their dinner ready. Will they be havin' the cold mutten from yisterday ma'a'm?" Her voice trailed down the hall.

Presently we heard the front door close. We raced to the top of the stairs.

"Is she gone?" we whispered, peering over the bannister into the hall below. But, of course, she was gone, else Mary Ellen would never dare to stand thus in the open doorway, gaping up and down the street! We slid recklessly down the hand-rail. It was the first infringement of rules—the wig was on the green! We crowded about Mary Ellen in the doorway, sniffing the air.

"Och, it's a bad lot ye are!" said she, taking The Seraph under the arms and swinging him out over the steps, "shure it's small wonder the missus is strict wid ye, else ye'd be ridin' rough-shod over her as ye do over me! It's jist man-nature, mind ye—ye can't help it!"

"Well, it's not man-nature to be mewed up as she does us," said Angel, swaggering, "and, I don't know what you mean to do, Mary Ellen, but we mean to take a day off, so there!" He nodded his curly head defiantly at her.

"Now, listen here, byes," said Mary Ellen, turning sober all of a sudden, and shutting the door, "you come right out to the kitchen wid me, an' we'll talk this thing over. I've got a word to say to ye."

She led the way down the hall and through the dining-room with its atmosphere of haircloth, into the more friendly kitchen, where even the oppressions of Mrs. Handsomebody could not quite subdue the bounding spirits of Mary Ellen.

Angel sallied to the cupboard. "Bother!" he said, discontentedly, investigating the cake-box, "that same old seedy-cake! Won't you please make us a treat today, Mary Ellen? Jam tarts or some sticky sort of cake like you see in the pastry shop window."

"That's the very thing I was goin' to speak about, my dear," Mary Ellen replied, "if ye'll jist howld yer horses." Before proceeding, she cut us each, herself included, a slice of the seed cake, and, when we were all munching (save Angel, who was busy picking the seeds out of his cake) she went on—

"Now, as well ye know, I've worked here manny a long month, and I've had followers a-plinty, yit there's noan o' thim I like the same as Mr. Watlin, the butcher's young man, an' it makes me blush wid shame, whin I think that after all the pippermints, an' gum drops, an' jawbone breakers he's give me, not to speak of minsthral shows

73

an' rides on the tram-cars, an' I've niver given him so much as a cup o' tay in this kitchen. Not wan cup o' tay, mind ye!"

We shook our heads commiseratingly. Angel flicked his last caraway seed at her—

"Well," he said, with a wink, "you gave him something better than tea—I saw you!"

"Aw, well, my dear," replied Mary Ellen, without smiling, "a man that do be boardin' all the time likes a little attintion sometimes—an' a taste o' home cookin'. Now hark to my plan. I mane to have a little feast of oyster stew, an' cake, an' coffee, an' the like this very night, fer Mr. Watlin an' me, an' yersilves. You kin have yours in the dining-room like little gintlemen, an' him an' me'll ate in the kitchen here. Thin, after the supper, ye kin come out an' hear Mr. Watlin play on the fiddle. He plays somethin' grand, 'havin' larned off the best masters. It'll be a rale treat fer ye! The missus 'll niver be the wiser, an' we'll all git a taste o' freedom, d'ye see?"

We were unanimous in our approval, The Seraph expressing his by a somersault.

"But," said Angel, "there's just one thing, Mary Ellen; if there's going to be a party you and Mr. Watlin have got to have yours in the dining-room the same as us. It'll be ever so much jollier, and more like a real party."

"Thrue fer ye, Master Angel!" cried Mary Ellen heartily, "sure, there's noan o' the stiff-neck about ye, an' ye'll git yer fill av oysters an' cake fer that, mark my words! As fer my Mr. Watlin, there ain't a claner, smarter feller to be found annywheres. But, oh, if the mistress was to find it out—" she turned pale with apprehension.

"How could she?" we assured her. Every curtain would be drawn, and, besides, Mrs. Handsomebody was not intimate with her neighbours.

Mary Ellen gave us our cold mutton and rice pudding that day in free and easy fashion. She did not place the dishes and cutlery with that mathematical precision demanded of her by Mrs. Handsomebody, but scattered them over the cloth in a promiscuous way that we found very exhilarating. And, instead of Mrs. Handsomebody's austere figure dominating our repast, there was Mary Ellen, resting her red knuckles on the table-cloth, and fairly

74

bubbling over with plans for the prospective entertainment of her lover! Our hearts went out to the good girl and her Mr. Watlin. We began to think of him as a dear friend.

"Now, my dears," said she, when the meal was over, "take yourselves off while I clane up and do my shoppin', but fer pity's sake, don't lave the front garden, fer if annything was to happen to ye—"

Angel cut her short with—"None of that Mary Ellen! This is our day too, and we shall do what we jolly well please!" He completed his protest by throwing himself bodily on the stout domestic, and The Seraph and I, though we had eaten to repletion, followed his example. Mary Ellen, howbeit, was a match for the three of us, and bundled us out of the side entrance into the laneway, triumphantly locking the door upon us.

Without a look behind, we scampered to the street, and then stood still, staring at each other, dazzled by the vista that opened up before us—what to do with these glorious hours of freedom!

II

It was one of those late February days, when Nature, after months of frozen disregard for man, of a sudden smiles, and you see that her face has grown quite young, and that she is filled with gracious intent towards you. The bare limbs of the chestnut trees before the house looked shiny against the dim blue of the sky; they seemed to strain upward toward the light and warmth. A score of sparrows were busy on the roadway.

After all, it was The Seraph who made the first dash, who took the bit in his milk-teeth, as it were; and, without a by-your-leave, strutted across the strip of sod to the road, and so set forth. He carried his head very high, and he would now and then shake it in that manner peculiar to the equine race. Angel and I followed closely with occasional caracoles, and cavortings, and scornful blowings through the nostrils. All three shied at a lamp-post. It needed no second glance to perceive that we were mettlesome steeds out for exercise, and feeling our oats.

A very old gentleman with an umbrella and top hat saw us. He rushed to the curb waving his umbrella and crying, "Whoa, whoa," but we only arched our proud necks and broke into a gallop. How the pavement echoed under our flying hoofs! How warmly the sun glistened on our sleek coats! How pleasant the jingling sound of the harness and the smell of the harness oil!

We left the decorous street we knew so well, and turned into narrow and untidy Henwood street. Shabby houses and shops were jumbled promiscuously together, and the pavement was full of holes. From the far end of it came the joyous tones of a hand-organ, vibrating on the early afternoon air. The eaves on the sunny side of the street were dripping. A fishmonger's shop sent forth its robust odour. The scarlet of a lobster caught our eyes as we flew past.

Could it be possible that the player of the organ was our old friend Tony, to whose monkey we had often handed our coppers through the palings?

We were horses no longer. Who had time for such pretence when Tony was grinding out "White Wings" with all his might? Angel and I took to the side-walk and ran with all speed, leaving the poor little Seraph pumping away in the rear, not quite certain whether he was horse or boy, but determined not to be outdistanced.

It was indeed Tony, and his white teeth gleamed when he saw us coming, and his eyebrows went up to his hat brim at sight of us bareheaded and alone, who always handed our coppers through the palings. And Anita, the monkey, was there, looking rather pale and sickly after the long Winter, but full of pluck, grinning, as she doffed her gold-braided hat.

Angel and The Seraph rarely had any money. The little allowance father gave us through Mrs. Handsomebody, burnt a hole in their pockets till it was expended on toffee or marshmallows. But I was made of different stuff, and by the end of the week, I was the financial strength of the trio. It was I, who now fished out a penny which Angel snatched from me. He craved the joy of the giver, and chuckled when Anita's small pink palm closed over the coin. But I was too happy to quarrel with him. Every one seemed in good-humour that day. Windows were pushed up and small change tossed out, or dropped in Anita's cup as she perched, chattering, on the sill. A stout grocer in his white apron gave her a little pink biscuit to nibble. Half-grown girls lolled on the handles of perambulators to listen, while their charges pulled faces of fear at the supple Anita.

We three sat on the curb close to the organ, our small heads reeling with the melodies that thundered from it. When Tony moved on, we rose and followed him. At the next corner he rested his organ on its one leg and looked down at us.

"You betta go home," he admonished, "your mamma not like."

"We're going to run the streets today," I said, manfully, "Mrs. Handsomebody is away at a funeral."

"A funer-al," repeated Tony, "she know—about dis?"

"No—" I replied, "but Mary Ellen does."

"She a beeg lady—dis Marie Ellen?"

"Oh, yes. She's awfully big. Bigger than you, and strong—"

"Oh, all right," said Tony, "but don' you get los'." We helped him to carry the organ. It was a new one he said, and very expensive to hire. We asked him endless questions we had always been wanting to ask—about Italy, and his parents, and sisters, and we told him about father in South America, and about the party that night for Mr. Watlin.

From street to street we wandered till we were gloriously and irrevocably lost. Angel and I helped to grind the organ and The Seraph even presented himself at doors with Anita's little tin cup in his hand. And either because he was so little or his eyelashes were so long, he never came back empty-handed. Tony seemed well content with our company.

So the afternoon sped on. Narrow alleys we played in, and wide streets, and once we passed through a crowded thoroughfare where we had to hug close to the organ, and once we met Tony's brother Salvator, who gave us each a long red banana.

At last Tony, looking down at us with a smile, said:

"Jus' one more tune here, then I tak' you home. See? De sun's gettin' low and dat little one's gettin' tired. I tak' you home in a minute."

We, remembering the party, were nothing loath. Poor Mary Ellen would be in a state by now, and our legs had almost given out.

This street was a quiet one. At the corner some untidy little girls danced on the pavement, while a group of boys stood by, loafing against the window of a small liquor shop, and occasionally scattering the girls by some threat of hair-pulling or kissing.

The western sky was saffron. The eaves, that had been dripping all day, now wore silent rows of icicles. Possibly the little girls danced to keep warm. The Seraph began to whimper.

"This air stwikes cold on my legs," he murmured.

I sat down beside him on the curb, and we snuggled together for warmth.

"Never mind, old sport," I whispered cheerily. "Just think of the goodies Mary Ellen's making for us! Pretty soon we'll be home."

While I strove to revive The Seraph's flagging spirits, Angel had strolled along the street to watch the little girls. He had an eye for the gentle sex even when their fairness was disguised by dirty pinafores and stiff pigtails. I did not see what happened, but above the noise of the organ I heard first, shouts of derision and anger, and then my brother's voice crying out in pain.

I pushed aside the clinging Seraph and ran to where I saw the two groups melted into one about a pair of combatants. The little girls parted to let me through. I saw then that the contending parties were Angel and a boy whose tousled head was fully six inches above my brother's. He had gripped Angel by the back of the neck with one hand, while with the other he struck blows that sounded horrible to me. Angel was hitting out wildly. When the boy saw me, he hooked his leg behind Angel's and threw him on his back with deadly ease, at the same time administering a kick in the stomach. He turned then to me with a leer.

"Well, pretty," he simpered, "does yer want some too? I s'y fellers, 'ere's another Hangel comin' fer 'is dose. Put up yer little 'ooks then; an' I'll give yer two black 'osses an' a red driver! Aw, come on, sissy!"

I tried to remember what father had said about fighting. "Don't clutch and don't paw. Strike out from the shoulder like a gentleman." So, while the boy was talking, I struck out from the shoulder right on the end of his nose with my shut fist.

Whatever things I may achieve, never, ah, never shall I experience a thrill of triumph equal to that which made my blood dance when I saw a trickle—a goodly, rich red trickle!—of blood spurt from the bully's nose.

"Ow! Ow! Wesley! Oo's got a red driver on 'is own?" shouted his comrades. "Plug aw'y little 'un!"

He snarled horribly, showing his big front teeth. I could feel his breath hot on my face as he clutched me round the neck. I could see some boys holding Angel back, I could hear The Seraph's wail of "John! John!" Then, simultaneously there came a blow on my own nose, and a grasping of my collar, and a shaking that freed us of each other, for I was clutching him with fury equal to his own.

A minute passed before I could regain possession of myself. The street reeled, the organ seemed to be grinding in my own head, and yet I found that it was not playing at all, for there was Tony with it on his back, looking anxiously into my face, and firing a volley of invective after the big boy, who was retreating with his mates.

I looked up at the owner of the hand which still held my collar. He was a very thin young man with a pale face and quiet grey eyes.

Tony began to offer incoherent explanations.

"But who are they?" demanded the young man, "they don't seem to belong to this street."

"No, no, no," reiterated Tony, "dey are little fr-riends of mine—dey come for a walk with me. Oh, I shall get into some trouble for dis, I tink! It was all dose damn boys dat bully heem, an' when I would run to help, dere was my Anita lef' on da organ, an' I mus' not lose her!"

"It's all right," I explained to the young man, "we were just spending the afternoon with Tony, and it wasn't his fault we got to fighting, and—and did I do very badly please? Did you notice whether I pawed or not?"

"By George!" said the young man, "you made the claret flow!"

"It took two of them to hold me or I'd have got back at him," said Angel.

"It took fwee o' them to hold me," piped The Seraph, "or I'd have punched evwybody!"

79

"How did it start?" enquired the young man.

"That biggest one asked me my name," replied Angel, "and before I thought I'd said, 'Angel,' and that started them. Of course my real name is David, but I forgot for the moment."

"Pet names are a nuisance sometimes," said the young man, smiling, "I had one once. It was John Peel. But no one calls me that now."

"I will tak' dem home now," interrupted Tony. "Come," taking The Seraph's hand, "dere will be no more running da street for you little boys!"

"I'll walk along, too," said the young man, "I've nothing else to do."

I strode along at his side greatly elated. I was as hot as fire, and some of the gamin's blood was still on my hand. I cherished it secretly.

Although the young man had quiet, even sad, eyes, it turned out that he was wonderfully interesting. He had travelled considerably, and had even visited South America, yet he could not have been an engineer like father, building railroads, for he looked very poor.

I was sorry when we reached Mrs. Handsomebody's front door.

"Good-bye," he said, holding out his hand.

But a happy thought struck me. I told him about Mary Ellen's party. "And," I hurried on, "there'll be oysters and coffee and all sorts of good things to eat, and we'd like most awfully to have you join us if you will. Mary Ellen would be proud to entertain a friend of ours. Wouldn't she Angel?"

"Yes, and Tony can come too!" cried Angel. "We'll have a regular party!"

"Yes, yes, I will come to da party," said Tony, quickly, "I am vera hungry. You will egsplain to Mees Marie Ellen, yes?"

"John can 'splain anything," put in The Seraph.

"Oh, please come!" I pleaded, dragging the young man down the side passage. He suffered himself to be led as far as the back entrance, but, once there, he halted.

80

"Tony and I shall wait here," he said, "and you'll go in and send your Mary Ellen out to inspect us. We shall see what she thinks of such a surprise party before we venture in, eh, Tony?" He gave a queer little laugh.

"Yes, yes," said Tony, "I will leave da organ out sida, but Anita mus' come in. She is vera good monk in a party."

III

We three entered breathlessly. Who can describe the babble of our explanations and appeals to Mary Ellen's hospitality, and her reproaches for the fright we had given her? Howbeit, when the first clamour subsided, we perceived that Mary Ellen's Mr. Watlin was ensconced behind the stove, looking tremendously dressed up and embarrassed. He now came forward and shook each of us by the hand, quite enveloping our little paws in a great expanse of warm thick flesh, smelling of scented soap.

The greetings over, Mary Ellen and he conferred for a moment in the corner, then Mr. Watlin creaked across the kitchen on tiptoe (I fancy he could not yet bring himself to believe in Mrs. Handsomebody's entire absence from the house) and disappeared through the outer door into the yard where the young man and Tony and Anita waited.

"Now," said Mary Ellen, sternly, "ye've just got to abide by Mr. Watlin's decision. If he says they're passable, why, in they come, an' if he gives 'em their walkin' ticket, well an' good, an' not a squeak out o' ye. I've had about enough o' yer actions for wan day!"

"But he's a gentleman, Mary Ellen!" I insisted.

"Ay, an' the monkey's a lady, no doubt! I know the kind!" I had never seen Mary Ellen so sour.

But our fears for our friends were set at rest, for at that instant, the door opened and Mr. Watlin entered, followed by the young man and Tony, with Anita perching on his shoulder. Mary Ellen could not refrain from a broad smile at the spectacle. The kitchen was filled with delightful odours. The spirits of everyone seemed to rise at a bound.

81

"Good-evening to ye, Tony," said Mary Ellen, and then she turned to our new friend.

"I don't know how you call yourself, sir," she said, bluntly.

"You may call me Harry, if you will," he replied, after a slight hesitation.

Mary Ellen, with a keen look at him, said, "Won't you sit down, sir? The victuals will be on the table in the dining-room directly. Mr. Watlin, would ye mind givin' me a hand with them dish-covers?"

Mr. Watlin assisted Mary Ellen deftly, and with an air of proprietorship. He was a stout young man with a blond pompadour, and a smooth-shaven ruddy face. As soon as an opportunity offered, I asked him whether he had brought his fiddle. He smiled enigmatically.

"You shall see wot you shall see, and 'ear wot you shall 'ear," he replied.

In time the great tureen (Mrs. Handsomebody's silver plated one) was on the table and the guests were bidden to "sit in." Mary Ellen, full of dignity, seated herself in Mrs. Handsomebody's place behind the coffee urn, while Mr. Watlin drew forward the heavy armchair, which since the demise of Mr. Handsomebody, had been occupied by no one save the Unitarian minister when he took tea with us. Angel and The Seraph and I were ranged on one side of the table, and Tony and Harry on the other. Anita sat on the chair behind Tony, and every now and again she would push her head under his arm and peer shyly over the table, or reach with a thin little claw toward a morsel of food he was raising to his mouth.

It would be impossible to conceive of seven people with finer appetites, or of a hostess more determined that her guests should do themselves injury from over-eating. Although two of our company were unexpected, there was more than enough for every one. The oysters were followed by a Bedfordshire pudding, potatoes, cold ham, celery, several sorts of pastry, oranges and coffee. It was when we reached the lighter portion of the feast that tongues were unloosed, and conviviality bloomed like an exotic flower in Mrs. Handsomebody's dining-room.

Mary Ellen placed a plateful of scraps on the floor before Anita.

82

She said, "That ought to stand to her, pore thing! She do be awful ganted."

"These 'ere fancies is wot tikes me," said Mr. Watlin, helping himself to his third lemon turnover. "Sub-stantial food is all right. I shouldn't care to do without meat and the like, but it's the fancies that seems to tickle all the w'y down. Sub-stantial foods is like hugs, but fancies might come under the 'ead of kisses—you don't know when you get enough on 'em, hey Tony? You lika da kiss?"

Tony turned up his palms.

"Oh, no, no, dey are not for a poor fella lak me!"

"Watlin," said Harry, "did you say you were a Kent man?"

"Ay, from Kent, the garden of England."

"Are you related to Carrot Bill Watlin, then?"

"Carrot Bill!" shouted Mr. Watlin, "Carrot Bill! Am I related to 'im? W'y 'e's my uncle, 'e is! And do you know 'im then?"

"I've seen him hundreds of times," said Harry.

"There never was such a feller as Carrot Bill," said Mr. Watlin, turning to us, "there ain't nobody in Kent can bunch carrots like 'im. W'y, truck-men from all over the county brings their carrots to Bill to be bunched, afore they tikes 'em to Covent Garden Market! 'E trims 'em down just so, an' fits 'em together till you'd think they'd growed in bunches. An' they look that 'andsome that they bring a penny more a bunch. An' to fancy you know 'im—well I never! Wot nime was it you said?"

"Harry."

"Ow, I meant your surnime."

"Smith," said Harry, shortly.

"Smith," meditated Mr. Watlin, "I know several Smiths in Kent. You're likely one on 'em. Well, I must shake 'ands with you for the sake of Carrot Bill." He reached across the table and grasped Harry's hand in a hearty shake. Thereupon we drank a health to Carrot Bill in bottled beer; and this was followed by a toast to Mrs. Handsomebody, which somehow subdued us a little.

"'Er brother is dead you s'y," reflected Mr. Watlin, "and 'ow hold a man might 'e be?"

"Blessed if I know," replied Mary Ellen, "but he was years an' years younger than her. She brought him up, and from what I can find out, he turned out pretty bad."

"Tck, tck." Mr. Watlin was moved. "It was very sad for the lidy, but 'e's dead now, poor chap! We must speak no ill of the dead."

"It's a vewy bad fing to be dead," interposed The Seraph, sententiously, "you can't eat, you can't dwink, an' you just fly 'wound an' 'wound, lookin' for somefing to light on!"

"Right-o, young gentleman!" said Mr. Watlin, "and put as couldn't be better. And the moral is, mike the most of our time wot's left!"

"Well, fer my part," sighed Mary Ellen, "I've et so hearty, I feel like as though I'd a horse settin' on my stomick! Sure I don't know how to move."

"A little pinch of bi-carbonate of soder will hease that, my dear," said her lover.

"Please, did you bring your fiddle, Mr. Watlin?" pleaded Angel, "won't you play now?"

"Ah, I lof da fiddle!" said Tony, caressing Anita's little head.

Mr. Watlin, thus importuned, disappeared for a space into the back hall, whence he finally emerged in his shirt sleeves, carrying the violin under his arm. We drew our chairs together at one end of the room, and watched him as he tuned the instrument, frowning sternly the while.

"Lydies and gentleman," said he, "I 'ope you'll pardon me appearing before you in my waistcoat. I must not be 'ampered you see, wen I manipulate the bow. I must 'ave freedom. It's a grand thing freedom! Ah!"

"He's gone as far as he can go on the fiddle," explained Mary Ellen to the company. "Someday he'll give up the butchering business and take to music thorough."

Mr. Watlin now, with the violin tucked under his chin, began to play in a very spirited manner. Our pulses beat time to lively polka and schottische while Mr. Watlin tapped on the carpet with his large foot as he played. Mary Ellen was wild for a dance, she said.

"Get up and 'ave a gow, then," encouraged Mr. Watlin, "you and 'Arry there!" But she, for some reason, would not, and Harry was not urgent.

"I can play da fiddle a little," said Tony, as our artist paused for a rest.

Mr. Watlin clapped him good-humouredly on the shoulder. "Go to it then, my boy, give us your little tune! I'm out of form tonight, anyw'y." He pushed the violin patronizingly into Tony's brown hands.

The Italian took it, oh, so lovingly, and, with an apologetic glance at Mr. Watlin, he tuned the strings to a different pitch. Anita climbed to the back of his neck.

Then came music, flooding, trickling, laughing, from the bow of Tony! Italy you could see; and little, half-naked children, playing in the sleepy street! You could hear the tinkle of donkey bells, and the cooing of pigeons; you could see Tony's home as he was seeing it, and hear his sisters singing. It was Spring in Tuscany.

The theme grew sad. It sang of loneliness. A lost child was wandering through the forest, who could not find his mother. It was very dark beneath the fir trees, and the wind made the boy shiver. His cry of—Mother! Mother! echoed in my heart and would not be hushed. I hid my face in the hollow of my arm and sobbed bitterly.

The music ceased. Harry had me in his arms.

"What's wrong, old fellow, was it something in Tony's music that hurt?"

I nodded, clinging to him.

"It's 'igh time 'e was in bed," said Mr. Watlin, taking the fiddle brusquely from the Italian's hands, "'e don't fancy doleful ditties, an' no more do I, hey Johnnie?"

Tony only smiled at me. "I tink you like my music," he said.

Harry now announced rather hurriedly that he must be going, and after he had said good-night to every one, and thanked Mary Ellen in a very manly way, he still kept my hand in his, and, together, we passed out of doors.

It was frosty cold. The air came gratefully to my hot cheeks. Harry stared up at the stars in silence for a moment, then he said:

"I want to tell you something, John, before I go. I don't know just how to make you understand. But I—I'm not the loafer you think I am—"

"Oh, I don't—"

"No one but a loafer or a sponge would do what I've done tonight," he persisted, "but I came here because I like you little chaps so well—and—because—I was so infernally hungry. I hadn't eaten since last night, you know, and when I heard about the oysters and coffee, I just couldn't refuse, and—I came."

"Oh, I'm sorry," I said, "I'm sorry, Harry! I like you awfully!"

I gave him my hand and, hearing the voices of Mr. Watlin and Tony, he hurried to the street.

I stumbled sleepily into the kitchen.

"Och, do go to bed, Masther John!" exclaimed Mary Ellen, "you're as white as a cloth! Well, if you're sick tomorrow, ye must jist grin an' bear it! An' sure we have had a day of it, haven't we? Thim oysters was the clane thing!"

IV

She followed us to the foot of the stairs with a lamp. The shadows of the bannisters raced up the wall ahead of us, as she moved away. The Seraph gripped the back of my blouse. We stopped at the door of Mrs. Handsomebody's bedroom. Like Mrs. Handsomebody, it towered above us, pale and forbidding.

"I dare you," said Angel, "to open it and stick your head in."

I was too drowsy to be timid. I turned the handle and opened the door far enough to insert my round tow head.

86

The room was unutterably still. A pale bluish light filtered through the long white curtains. The ghostly bed awaited its occupant. The door of a tall wardrobe stood open—did something stir inside? I withdrew my head and closed the door. Now I remembered that the room had smelled of black kid gloves. I shuddered.

"You were afraid!" jeered Angel.

"Not I. It was nothing to do."

But when we were safe in bed and Mary Ellen had come and put out our light, I lay a-thinking of the empty room. Strange, when people went away and left you, how Something stayed behind! A shadowy, wistful something, that smelled of kid gloves!

We slept till ten next morning. Mary Ellen superintended our baths. We were in a state to behold, she said, and she was apprehensive lest Mrs. Handsomebody should observe my swollen nose, for the big boy's fist had somewhat enlarged that unobtrusive feature.

"Jist say ye've a bit of feverish cold if she remarks it," she cautioned, "people often swells up wid colds."

We ate our bread and strawberry jam and milk from one end of the dining table. We heaped the bread with sugar, and stirred the jam into our milk. After breakfast, we played at knights and robbers in the schoolroom. It was a raw morning, and a Scotch mist dimmed the window pane.

Angel and I were in the midst of a terrific fight over a princess whom he was bearing off to his robber cave (The Seraph, draped in a chenille table-cover, impersonating the princess) when we were interrupted by the tinkle of the dinner bell.

How the morning had flown! Had she returned then? Was the funeral over? Had she heard our shouts? We descended the stairs with some misgivings and entered the dining-room in single file.

Yes, she was there, standing by the table, her black dress looking blacker than ever! After a dry little kiss on each of our foreheads, she motioned us to seat ourselves, and took her own accustomed place behind the tea things. There was a solemn click of knives and forks. Mary Ellen waited on us primly. It was not to be thought that this was the same room in which we had feasted so uproariously on the night previous.

Yet I stared at Mrs. Handsomebody and marvelled that she should suspect nothing. Did she get no whiff of the furry smell of Anita? Did no faint echo of Tony's music disturb her thoughts? What were her thoughts? Deep ones I was sure, for her brow was knit. Was she thinking of that brother on whom the Scotch mist was falling so remorselessly?

The Seraph was speaking.

"It's a vewy bad fing to be dead," he was saying reminiscently—, "you can't eat, you can't dwink, an' you jus' fly awound lookin' for somefing to light on!"

I trembled for him, but Mrs. Handsomebody, lost in thought, gave no heed to him.

At last she raised her eyes.

"I hope you behaved yourselves well, and made profitable use of your time during my absence?"

We made incoherent murmurs of assent.

"Name the Channel Islands, John."

"Guernsey, Jersey, Alderney, Sark, and Herm," I replied glibly. So much had I saved from the wreck of things ordained.

"Correct. Are you through your dinners then? You may pass out. Ah, your nose, John; it looks quite red. What caused that?"

I said that I believed I had an inward burning fever. I had embellished Mary Ellen's suggestion.

"I hope you are not going to be ill," she sighed.

It was not until Angel and I were back in the schoolroom, that we discovered the absence of The Seraph. We turned surprised looks on each other. Our junior seldom left our heels.

"I remember now," reflected Angel, "that, as he passed her, she stopped him. I didn't think anything of it. What can she have found out? D'you s'pose she's pumping the kid?"

We were left to our conjectures for fully a quarter of an hour. Then we heard him plodding leisurely up the stairs. We greeted him impatiently.

"What's up? Did you blab? Whatever did she say?" We hurled the questions at him.

The Seraph maintained an air of calm superiority. He even hopped from one floral wreath on the carpet to another, with his hands behind his back, as was his custom when he wished to reflect undisturbed. He ignored our importunities.

Angel, in exasperation, took him by the collar.

"You tell us why she kept you down there so long!"

Thus cornered, The Seraph raised his large eyes to our inquiring faces with great solemnity.

"She kept me," he said, "to cuddle me, an' to give me this—" he showed a white peppermint lozenge between his little teeth.

To cuddle him. Was the world coming to an end?

"Yes," he persisted, "she kept me to cuddle me, an' she was cwyin'— so there!"

Mrs. Handsomebody crying!

"It's about her dead brother, of course," said Angel. "That's why she cried."

"No," said The Seraph, stoutly. "He was a man, an' she was cwyin' about a little wee boy like me, she used to cuddle long ago!"

Chapter VI

D'ye Ken John Peel?

I

Probably a little boy is never quite so happy as when he is worshipping and imitating a young man. From this time on my hero was Harry, about whom so fascinating an air of mystery hung that his lightest word was something to be treasured. I pictured him, hungry and alone, perhaps brooding over the Collect for next Sunday, or something of equal melancholy. I was always on the watch for his tall, slender figure, when we took our walks, but when we did meet again, it came as a surprise, and quite took me off my feet.

A month had passed since Mary Ellen's party. It was a windy, sunny day in March, and great white clouds billowed in a clear sky—like clean clothes in a tub of blueing, Mary Ellen had said. I was sitting alone on the steps of the Cathedral. Angel was in the schoolroom writing his weekly letter to father, and The Seraph was suffering a bath at the hands of Mary Ellen, following an excursion into the remoter depths of the coal cellar.

So I sat on the Cathedral steps alone. It was a fine morning for flights of the imagination. The soft thunder of the Cathedral organ became at my will the booming of the surf on a distant coral reef. The pigeons wheeling overhead became gulls, whimpering in the cordage. Little did the ancient caretaker reck, as he swept the stretch of flagging before the carved door, that he was washing off the deck of a frigate, whilst I, the rover of the seas, kept a stern eye on him. Louder boomed the surf—then soft again. The door behind me had opened and closed. The deck-washer touched his cap. Then the Bishop stood above me, smiling, the sun glinting in his blue eyes and on the buttons of his gaiters.

"Hal-lo, John," he said. "What's the game this morning. Seafaring as usual?"

I nodded, "She's as saucy a frigate," I answered happily, "as ever sailed the seas, and this here wild weather is just a frolic for her. But

I don't like the look of yon black craft to the windward." And I pointed to a dustman's cart that had just hove into view.

"I entirely agree with you," replied the Bishop. "She looks as though she were out on dirty business. I'd like nothing better than to stay and see you make short work of her, but here it is Friday morning, and not a blessed word of my sermon written, so I must be getting on." And with that he strode down the street to his own house. I was alone again watching the approaching vessel with suspicion. Then, above the thrashing of the spray, I heard my name spoken by a voice I knew, and turning looked straight up into Harry's face.

"John!" he repeated. "What luck. I have been watching for you for days, you little hermit!"

"Watching for me, Harry?"

"Yes," he proceeded, "and the one time I saw you, that starched governess of yours had you gripped by the hand—"

—"just like any old baby girl," I broke in.

Harry laughed and shook my hand enthusiastically. I saw that he was even thinner than before. Was he, I wondered, "infernally hungry" at this very minute?

"John," he said, looking into my eyes: "You can help me if you will. We're friends, aren't we?"

I let him see that I was all on fire to help him, and it was then that he made his wonderful suggestion.

"Would it be possible to evade your governess long enough to come and have a bite with me?"

Dinner with Harry! In his own room! What an adventure to repeat to Angel and The Seraph! Without further parley I set off down Henwood street at a trot lest Mrs. Handsomebody should spy me from her bedroom window, in a fateful way she had. Harry hurried after me, catching my arm and drawing me close to him.

"What a plucky little shaver you are, John," he said. "I know she's a corker, but I think you and I are a match for her, eh?"

I strode beside him breathless. I felt taller, stronger, than ever before. By contrast with our masculinity Mrs. Handsomebody seemed a rather pitiful old woman.

We spoke little, but hurried through many streets, till, at last, we came to the narrow dingy one where I had first seen Harry. We turned down an alley beside a green grocer's shop and entered a narrow doorway into the strangest passage I had ever seen.

It was damp and chill. The floor was paved with dark red bricks and the walls were stone. On our left I glimpsed a dim closet where a woman with fat arms was dipping milk out of what looked like a zinc-covered box. On our right rose the steepest, most winding staircase imaginable; and close to the wall beside the stairs towered a giant grapevine whose stem was as thick as a man's arm. After an eccentric curve or two, this amazing vine disappeared through a convenient hole in the roof. I was lost in admiration and should have liked to stop and examine it, but Harry urged me up the stairs.

"How is that for steep?" he demanded, at the top. "Winded, eh? Now these are my digs, John—" and he threw open a door with a flourish.

It was a shabby little room with a threadbare carpet, yet it wore an air of adventure somehow. The lamp shade had a daring tilt to it; the blind had been run up askew; and the red table cover had been pushed back to make room for a mound of books. Harry's bed looked as though he had been having a pillow fight. Surely not with the fat lady downstairs.

Harry was clearing the table by tossing the books into the middle of the bed. "We're going to have tea directly," he explained. "Can't you hear her puffing up the stairs? I expect a catastrophe every time she does it." He set two chairs at the table and gazed eagerly at the doorway.

She appeared at last with heaving bosom carrying a large tray, and began to lay the table. I observed with great interest that she was placing a whole kidney for each of us, and that there were also potato chips and six jam puffs. Harry bade me sit down with the air of one who entertains a guest of importance; I swelled with pride as I attacked the kidney.

Harry, sitting opposite, eating with a gusto equal to my own, seemed to me the most perfect and luckiest of mortals.

"Harry!" I got it out through my mouth full of potato chips, "Harry, I say! Do you always have jolly things like these to eat?"

He gave a short laugh.

"Oh, no, my John! On the contrary there are many times when I do not eat at all. However, I paid a visit to an uncle of mine yesterday, who gave me so much money that I shall live well for some time to come, but—I shall never know the time o'day."

"Oh, but that's fine—" I cried, "Not to know the time! I wish I didn't for it's always time to go to bed, or do lessons, or take a tiresome walk with Mrs. Handsomebody."

Harry stared hard at me. "What do you suppose," he asked, "she'll do to you, for skipping dinner? Something pretty hot?"

"I dunno," I returned. "It's a new sort of badness. P'raps I'll have to do without tea, or maybe she'll write to father—she's always threatening. Don't let's talk about it."

"She appears to be a rather poisonous old party," commented Harry. "I see that it behooves me to get to business and tell you just why I brought you here." He pushed back his plate and took from his pocket a short thick pipe and lighted it.

"Now John," he smiled, "just finish up those jam puffs. Don't leave one, or my landlady will eat it, and she has double chins enough. I want to talk to you as man to man."

Man to man! How I wished that Angel could see me, being made the confidant of Harry! I helped myself to my third jam puff with an air of cool deliberation.

"Now—" Harry leant across the table, his eyes on mine, "What sort of looking man would you expect my father to be, John?"

I studied Harry and hazarded—"A brown face, and awfully thin, and greenish eyes, and crinkly brown hair."

"Wrong!" cried Harry, smiting the table. "My father's got a full pink face, the bluest of eyes and a fine head of white hair, which, I am afraid I helped to whiten, worse luck!"

"He sounds nice," I commented.

93

"He is. Now what do you suppose my father does, John?"

"Not a pirate!" but I said it hopefully.

"Far from it. He's a bishop."

"Hurray!" I cried. "Our best friend is a bishop. He lives right next door to us."

"The very man," said Harry. "He's my father."

I was incredulous.

"But he's only got his niece, Margery, and his butler, and his cook! The cook's awfully good to him. Makes his favorite pudding any day he wants it."

"Ay, but he's got me too," said Harry solemnly, "or, at least, he should have me. We're at the outs."

"Well, then, all you have to do is to make friends, isn't it?"

"Not so simple as it sounds," replied Harry gloomily.

"I have been a bad son to him." He rose abruptly and began walking up and down the room. I got to my feet too, and strode beside him, hands deep in pockets. I longed for a short thick pipe.

"I never did what he wanted me to," pursued Harry. "He wanted me to stick at college and make something of myself, but all I cared to do was to knock about with chaps who weren't good for me, and I simply wouldn't study. So we had words. Hot ones too. I left home with a little money my mother had left me. I was twenty-one then—five years ago." He looked down in my face with his sudden smile. "You're a rum little toad," he said. "I like to talk to you, John."

I thought: "When I'm a man I'll have a pipe like that, and hold it in my teeth when I talk."

Harry sat down on the side of his tumbled bed clasping an ankle.

"For three years," he went on, "I knocked about from one country to another seeing the world, till at last all my money was gone. Then I came back to England but I wouldn't go to my father until I had done something that would justify myself—make him proud of me. It seemed to me that I could become a great actor if I had a chance.

94

Very well. After a lot of waiting and disappointments I got an engagement with a third rate company that travelled mostly on one-night stands—you understand?

"I have been at it ever since, playing all sorts of parts—companies breaking up without salaries being paid—then another just as bad—cheap lodgings—bad food—and long stretches of being out of a job altogether. I am that way now. I have only seen my father once in all this time. It was simply—well—" He gave his funny smile and shook his head ruefully.

I leaned over the foot of the bed staring expectantly.

"We had arrived one Sunday morning in a small town, and were trailing wearily down the street just as the people were going to morning service. Suddenly, as I was passing a large church, I saw my father alight from the carriage at the door. I found out afterwards that he had come to conduct a special service. He was so near that I could have touched him, but I just stood, rooted to the spot, so beastly ashamed you know, with my shabby travelling bag behind me, and my heart pounding away like Billy-ho!"

"Oh, I wish he'd seen you!" I cried, "he'd have made it up like a shot."

Harry blew a great cloud of smoke. "Well, I want to sneak back to him, John—but—here's the rub—perhaps Margery does not want me." He sucked gloomily at his pipe for a bit in silence, then taking it from his mouth he stabbed at me with the stem of it.

"This is where you come in my friend. You'd like to help, wouldn't you?"

I nodded emphatically.

"This, then, is what I want you to do. Find Margery this afternoon and say to her: 'Margery, I've met your cousin Harry. Would you like to have him come home again?' Watch her face then—you're a shrewd little fellow—and if she looks happy and pleased about it you must let me know, but if she looks glum and as if her plans had been upset, you must tell me just the same. Never mind what she says, watch her face. Will you do it?"

"Rather!" We shook hands on it.

95

"But—" I asked, "when shall I see you? I daren't come here again, I'm afraid."

"Tomorrow is Saturday," he replied thoughtfully. "The Bishop will keep to his study till noon—"

"And Mrs. Handsomebody goes to market!" I chimed in.

"Good. I'll be at the Cathedral corner at ten o'clock. Meet me there. Now you'd better cut home."

He took my arm and led me down the strange winding stairway, through the cool damp passage where the grapevine grew, to the sunken doorstep.

"Know your way home?" he demanded. "Right-o! I depend on you, John. And mind you watch her face, like a cat. Good-bye!" And he affectionately squeezed my arm.

II

I set off as fast as my legs could carry me; and the nearer home I drew, the greater became my fear of Mrs. Handsomebody. What would she say? Dinner would be over long ago I knew. My steps began to lag as I reached the Cathedral corner. The great grey pile usually so friendly now rose before me gloomily. Inside, the organ boomed like an accusing voice. My heart sank. Mrs. Handsomebody's house with the blinds drawn three-quarters of the way down the windows seemed to watch my approach with an air of cold cynicism.

Softly I turned the door-knob and entered the dim hall. All was quiet, a quiet pervaded by the familiar smell of old fabrics, bygone meals, and umbrellas. The white door of the parlour towered like a ghost. I put my arm across my eyes and began to cry.

At first I only snivelled, but surrendered myself after a few successful ventures, to a loud despairing roar.

I could see the blurred image of Mrs. Handsomebody standing at the top of the stairs. I heard her sharp command to mount them instantly, and I began to grope my way up, hanging by the bannister.

96

When I had gained the top, her angular hand grasped my shoulder and pushed me before her, into the schoolroom. The Seraph's eyes were large with sympathy, but Angel grinned maliciously. Our governess seated herself beside her desk and placed me in front of her.

"Now," she said, in a voice of cold anger, "will you be good enough to explain your strange conduct? Where have you been all this while?"

"Sittin' on the Cathedral steps," I sobbed.

"That is a falsehood, John. Twice I sent David to search for you there and both times he reported that you were nowhere in sight. Where were you? Answer truthfully or it will be the worse for you."

"I h-hid when I saw him comin'," I stammered, "I was too s-sick to come home." Surely this would affect her!

She stared incredulously. "Sick! Where are you sick?"

"All o-ver."

"Take your hand from your eyes. What made you sick?"

"I f-fell."

"Fell!" her tone was contemptuous. "Where did you fall?"

"D-down."

Mrs. Handsomebody became ironical.

"How extraordinary! I have never heard of people falling up."

"They can fall out," interrupted Angel.

Mrs. Handsomebody rapped her ruler in his direction.

"Silence!" she gobbled. "Not another word from you." Then, turning to me—"You say that you fell down, hurt yourself, and have since been in hiding. Now tell me precisely what happened from the moment that you ventured beyond the bounds I have prescribed for you."

There was no use in hedging. I saw that there was nothing for it but to drown this woman out; so I raised my voice and drowned her out.

My next sensation was that of a scuffle, several sharp smacks with the ruler, and at last being sat down very hard on a chair in our bedroom. Mrs. Handsomebody was standing in the doorway. I had never seen her with so high a colour.

"You will remain in that chair," she commanded, "until tea time. Do not loll on the bed. And you may rest assured that I shall leave no stone unturned till I have discovered every detail of this prank. It is at such times as these that I regret ever having undertaken the charge of three such unruly boys. It is only the high regard in which I hold your father that makes it tolerable. I hope you will take advantage of your solitude to review thoroughly your past."

She closed the door with deliberate forebearance, then I heard the key click in the lock and her inexorable retreating footsteps.

I found my wad of a handkerchief and rubbed my cheeks. I had stopped crying but my body still was shaken. For a long time I sat staring straight before me busy with plans for the afternoon. Then I fell asleep.

A soft thumping on the panel of the door roused me at last. I felt stiff and rather desolate.

"John!" It was The Seraph's voice. "I say, John! You should be a dwagon, an' when I kick on the door you should woar fwightfully."

"Where's she?" 'Twas thus we designated our governess.

"Gone away out. Will you be a dwagon, John?"

Obligingly I dropped to my hands and knees and ambled to the door. The Seraph kicked it vigorously and I began to roar. I was pleased to find that so much crying had left my voice very husky so that I could indeed roar horribly. The louder The Seraph kicked the louder I roared. It was exhausting, and I had had about enough of it when I heard Mary Ellen pounding up the uncarpeted back stairs.

"If you kick that dure onct more—" she panted—"ye little tormint—I'll put a tin ear on ye! As fer you, Masther John, 'tis yersilf has a voice like young thunder!"

She unlocked the door and threw it wide open; Angel and The Seraph crowded in after her. Mary Ellen's sleeves were rolled above her elbows, her red face was covered with little beads of perspiration, and she wore large goloshes. A savour of soap suds, mops, and the corners of old pantries, emanated from her. She extended to me a moist palm on which lay a thick slice of bread spread with cold veal gravy.

"This," said she, "is to stay ye till tea-time; an' now let me git back to me scrubbin' or the suds'll be all dried up on me."

But I caught her apron and held her fast.

"Oh, don't go, Mary Ellen!" I begged, "I've something awfully interesting to tell you. Do sit down!"

"I will not thin. And you've nothin' to tell me that I haven't got be heart already."

"But this is about Harry, who had supper with us and Mr. Watlin and Tony. It's a most surprising adventure. Just wait and hear." I dragged her to a chair.

She settled back with a smile of relaxation. "Aw well," she remarked, "who would be foriver workin' fer small pay an' little thanks? Out wid your story my lambie." And she drew The Seraph on her ample lap.

So while they clustered about me I told my whole adventure, ending with Harry's plea that I interview Margery on his behalf.

"It's a 'normous responsibility," I sighed.

"Don't you worry," said Mary Ellen, "she'll want him home fast enough, a fine young gintleman like him. Now I'm minded of it, their cook did tell me that the Bishop had a son that was a regular playboy."

"He's not a playboy," I retorted. "He's splendid—and please Mary Ellen, there's something I want you to do for me. You must let me go this minute to see Margery and find out if she wants him back again."

"Oh, she'll have him, no fear." This with a broad smile.

"But I've got to ask her. I promised. It's a 'normous responsibility. Will you please let me, Mary El-len?"

"I will not," replied Mary Ellen, firmly. "It'ud be as much as my place is worth."

99

I began to cry. Angel came to the rescue.

"Be a sport, Mary Ellen. Let him go. I'll stand at the gate and if I see the Dragon coming, I'll pass the tip to John, and he can cut over the garden wall and be in the room before she gets to the front door."

Mary Ellen threw up her hands. She never could resist Angel's coaxing. "God save Ireland," she groaned, and, dropping The Seraph, clattered back to the kitchen.

The Seraph stood like a rumpled robin where she had deposited him. He had confided to me once that he rather liked being nursed by Mary Ellen, though the heaving of her bosom bothered him. He was far too polite to tell her this: but now that she was gone, he hunched his shoulders, stretched his neck and breathed—

"What a welief!—"

I found Margery alone in the drawing-room. People had just been, for teacups were standing about, and a single muffin lay in a silver muffin dish. Even in the stress of my mission its isolation appealed to me.

Margery was doing something to a bowl of roses but she looked up, startled at my appearance.

"Why, John!" she exclaimed, "what is the matter with you? Have you been crying? Your face is awfully smudgy."

"Sorry," I replied, "I wasn't crying but I'm on very particular business and I hadn't time to wash." I went at it, hammer and tongs, then—"It's about Harry. He wants to know if you'll have him home again."

Margery looked just puzzled.

"Harry! Harry who?"

"Your Harry," I replied, manfully. "The Bishop's Harry." And I poured out the whole story of my meeting with Harry and his passionate desire to come home. All the while, I anxiously watched Margery's face for signs of joy or disapproval. It was pale and still as the face of a white moth, but when she spoke her words fell on my budding hopes like cold rain. She put her hands on my shoulders and said earnestly:

"You must tell him not to come, John. It would be such a great pity! The Bishop is quite, quite used to being without him now, and it would upset him dreadfully to try to forgive Harry. I don't believe he could. And he and I are so contented. Harry would be very disturbing—you see, he's such a restless young man, John; and he hasn't been at all kind to his father. He's done—things—"

"But you don't know him!" I interrupted. "He's splendid!"

"I don't want to know him," Margery persisted. "He's a very—"

I could let this thing go no further. Here was another woman who must be drowned out. I raised my voice, therefore, and almost shouted—

"Well, you've got to know him! He's coming home tomorrow night. At seven. He wants his bed got ready. So there."

Margery sat down. She got quite red.

"Why didn't you tell me this before?" she demanded.

"'Cos I was breaking it to you gently, like they do accidents," I answered calmly.

Suddenly Margery began to laugh hysterically. She pressed her palms against her cheeks and laughed and laughed. Then she said:—

"John, you're a most extraordinary boy."

I thought so too, but I said, modestly—"Oh, well. Somebody had to do it." Then, in the flush of my triumph I remembered Mrs. Handsomebody. "But, oh, I say, I must be going! And—please— would it matter much if we were here to see him come home? We'd be very quiet."

Margery looked relieved. "I believe it would help—" she said. "It will be rather difficult. Yes, do come. Ask your governess if you may spend an hour with Uncle and me between your tea and bedtime. And, oh, John, that muffin looks wretchedly lonely."

Outside, I divided the spoils with Angel.

"Well—" he demanded, his mouth full of muffin— "shewanimbagagen?"

"Rather," I cried, joyously. "I managed the whole thing. And we're to be there at seven to see him come."

We raced to the kitchen and told Mary Ellen, who was promptly impressed, but The Seraph after a close scrutiny of us, said bitterly—

"There's cwumbs on your faces!"

"Cwumbs on your own face, old sillybilly!" mocked Angel, "and what's more, they're sugar cwumbs!"

III

As fate would have it, Mrs. Handsomebody decreed that I should not leave the house on Saturday morning, and she, having a spell of sciatica did not go to market, as usual; so there I was, unable to meet Harry on the cathedral steps, as I had promised. It simply meant that Angel must undertake the mission, while I kicked my heels in the schoolroom.

He undertook it with a careless alacrity that was very irritating to one who longed to finish, in his own fashion, an undertaking that had, so far, been carried on with masterly diplomacy.

The Seraph went with Angel, and it seemed a long hour indeed till I heard the longed-for footsteps hurrying up the stairs. The door was thrown open, and they burst in rosy and wind-blown.

"It's all right," announced Angel briskly. "He'll be there sharp at seven, and he's jolly glad that we're to be there too!"

"And did you tell him?" I asked rather plaintively, "that I had done the whole thing?"

"Course I did."

"What did he say when you told him he was to come home?"

"He slapped his leg—" Angel gave his own leg a vigorous slap in illustration—"and said—'once aboard the lugger, and the girl is mine!'"

It was a fascinating and cryptic utterance. We all tried it on varying notes of exultation. It put zest into what otherwise would have been a dragging day. By tea-time our legs were sore with whacking.

Came the hour at last. We set out holding each other by moist clean hands, an admonishing Mrs. Handsomebody on the doorsill.

Our hearts were high with excitement when we were shown ceremoniously into the Bishop's library, where he and Margery were sitting in the dancing firelight. We loved the dark-panelled room where we were always made so happy. At Mrs. Handsomebody's we could never do anything right, mugs of milk had a spiteful way of tilting over on the table-cloth without ever having been touched, but we could handle the things in the Chinese cabinet here or play carpet ball on the rug in the most seemly fashion.

No one could tell stories like the Bishop, and after we had played for a bit, and The Seraph had demonstrated, on the hearthrug, how he could turn a somersault, some one suggested a story.

I often thought it a pity that those, who only heard the Bishop preach, should never know how his great talents were wasted in that rôle. It took the "Arabian Nights" to bring out the deep thrill of his sonorous voice, and his power of filling the human heart with delicious fear.

Now we perched about him listening with rapt eyes to the tale of Ali Baba. We wished there were more women like the faithful Morgiana with her pot of boiling oil. The Seraph, especially, revelled in the thought of those poor devils of thieves, each simmering away in his own jar.

There fell a silence when the story was finished, and I was just casting about in my mind for the next one I should beg, when, Angel, looking at the clock, suddenly asked:

"Bishop, will you sing? Will you please sing us a nice old song 'stead of a story? Sing 'John Peel,' won't you?"

"Please sing 'John Peel'!" echoed The Seraph.

The Bishop seemed loath to sing "John Peel." It was years since he had sung it, he said; he had almost forgotten the words. But when Margery joined her persuasions to ours, he consented to sing just one verse and the chorus. So he sang (but rather softly);

"D'ye ken John Peel, with his coat so grey?
D'ye ken John Peel, at the break of day?
D'ye ken John Peel, when he's far, far away,
With his hounds and his horn in the morning?"

Before he had time to begin the chorus, it was taken up by a mellow baritone voice in the hall. It began softly too,˙but when it reached the "View halloo," it rang boldly.

"For the sound of his horn brought me from my bed,
And the cry of his hounds, which he oft-times led,
Peel's 'View halloo!' would awaken the dead,
Or the fox from his lair in the morning."

The Bishop never moved a muscle till the last note died away, then he shook us off him, took three strides to the door, and swept the curtains back. Harry stood in the doorway with a rather shame-faced smile.

"Good God!" exclaimed the Bishop. "Harry!" Then he put his arms around him and kissed him.

I threw a triumphant glance at Margery. It hadn't hurt the Bishop at all to forgive Harry.

"It was all the doing of these kids," Harry was saying, "if they hadn't cleared the way, I'd never have dared. John engineered everything. As a diplomat he's a pocket marvel."

He and Margery gave each other a very funny look. I should like to have heard their later conversation.

"They're good boys," said the Bishop, with an arm still around Harry, "capital boys, and if their governess will let them come to dinner tomorrow we'll have a sort of party, and talk everything over. I think cook would make a blackberry pudding. Will you arrange it Margery? Just now I want—" He said no more, but he and Harry gripped hands.

Margery herded us gently into the hall, and gave us each two chocolate bars.

Going home under the first pale stars, we were three rollicking blades indeed. We no longer held hands, but we hooked arms, and swaggered and we did not ring the bell till the last vestige of chocolate was gone.

As we waited for Mary Ellen, I said, suddenly to Angel:

"Angel, what made you ask the Bishop to sing 'John Peel'? Did you know Harry was going to sing in the hall?"

"Oh, Harry and I fixed that up this morning," replied my senior, airily. "I kept it to myself, 'cos I didn't want any interference, see?"

Mary Ellen, opening the door at this moment, prevented a scuffle, though I was in too happy a mood to quarrel with any one.

Mrs. Handsomebody was surprisingly civil about our visit. She showed great interest in the return of the Bishop's only son. Was he a nice young man? she asked. Was he nice-looking? Did the Bishop appear to be overjoyed to see him?

We three were seated on three stiff-backed chairs, our backs to the wall. Angel and I told her as much as was good for her to know of the adventure.

The Seraph felt that he was being ignored, so when a pause came, he remarked in that throaty little voice of his:

"It's a vewy bad fing to be boiled in oil."

"What's that?" snapped Mrs. Handsomebody. "Say that again!"

"It's a vewy bad fing to be boiled in oil," reiterated The Seraph suavely, "thirty-nine of 'em there was—for the captain was stabbed alweady—boilin' away in oil. Their ears was full of it."

Mrs. Handsomebody gripped the arms of her chair, and leaned towards him.

"Alexander, I have never known a child of such tender years to possess so unquenchable a lust for frightfulness. It must be eradicated at all costs."

The Seraph stood, then, balancing himself on the rung of his chair,

"'Once aboard the lugger,'" he sang out, slapping his plump little thigh, "'and the gell is mine!'"

Mrs. Handsomebody sank back in her chair. She said:

"This is appalling. David—John—take your little brother to bed instantly! Take him out of my hearing."

105

Angel and I each grasped an arm of the reluctant infant and dragged him from the room. He stamped up the stairway between us, with an air of stubborn jollity.

When we had reached the top, he loosed himself from me and put his head over the handrail.

"'John Peel's View Halloo! would waken the dead'—" he roared down into the hall.

But he got no further. Between us we hustled him into the bedroom, and shut the door. Angel and I leaned against it, then, in helpless laughter.

In a moment I felt my arm squeezed by Angel, who was pointing ecstatically toward the bed.

There, by the bedside, his dimpled hands folded, his curly head meekly bent, knelt The Seraph.

He was saying his prayers.

Chapter VII

Granfa

I

At Mrs. Handsomebody's on a Sunday morning Angel and I had an egg divided between us, after our porridge. It was boiled rather hard so that it might not run, and we watched the cutting of it jealously. The Seraph's infant organs were supposed not to be strong enough to cope with even half an egg, so he must needs satisfy himself with the cap from Mrs. Handsomebody's; and he made the pleasure endure by the most minute nibbling, filling up the gaps with large mouthfuls of toast.

It was at a Sunday morning breakfast that Mrs. Handsomebody broached the subject of fishing. Angel and I had just scraped the last vestige of rubbery white from our half shells, and, having reversed them in our egg-cups, were gazing wistfully at what appeared to be two unchipped eggs, when she spoke.

"You have been invited by Bishop Torrance to go on a fishing excursion with him tomorrow, and I have consented; provided, of course, that your conduct today be most exemplary. What do you say? Thanks would not be amiss."

Angel and I mumbled thanks, though we were well nigh speechless with astonishment and joy. The Seraph bolted his cherished bit of egg whole and said in his polite little voice:

"He's a vewy nice man to take us fishin'. I wonder what made him do it."

"I have never pretended," returned Mrs. Handsomebody, stiffly, "to account for the vagaries of the male. Yet I grant you it seems singular that a dignitary of the church should find pleasure in such a project, in company with three growing boys."

"If it had been anyone but the Bishop," she went on, "I should have refused, for there are untold possibilities of danger in trout fishing. You must, for example, guard against imbedding the fish hook in the flesh, which is most painful, often leading to blood-poisoning.

107

This is to say nothing of the risk in sitting on damp grass, or the stings of insects."

"Did you ever sit on the sting of an insect, please?" questioned The Seraph eagerly.

Mrs. Handsomebody looked at him sharply. "One more question of that character," she said, "and you will remain at home." Then, glancing around the table, she went on—"What! your eggs gone so soon? We shall give thanks then. Alexander"—to The Seraph—"It is your turn to say grace. Proceed."

The Seraph, with folded hands and bent head, repeated glibly:

"Accept our thanks, O Lord, for these Thy good cweatures given to our use, and by them fit us for Thy service. Amen."

There was a scraping of chairs, and we got to our feet. The Seraph, holding his bit of egg shell in his warm little palm asked—"Is an egg a cweature, yet?"

Mrs. Handsomebody gloomed down at him from her height. "I say it in all solemnity, Alexander, the natural bent of your mind is toward the ribald and cynical. I do what I can to curb it, but I fear for your future." And she swept from the room.

Eagerly we took our places in the choir stalls that morning.

The May sunshine had taken on the mellowness of summer, and it struck fire from the sacred vessels on the altar, and the brazen-winged eagle of the lectern. Strange-shaped patterns of wine-colour and violet were cast from the stained glass windows upon the walls and pillars, enriching the grey fabric of the church, like tropic flowers. The window nearest me was a favourite of ours. It was dedicated, so saith the bronze tablet beneath, to the memory of Cosmo John, fifth son of an Earl of Aberfalden. He had died at the age of fifteen, not a tender age to me, but the age toward which I was eagerly straining, the vigourous, untrammelled age of the big boy.

I stared at the young knight in the red cloak who, to me, represented Cosmo John, and thought it a great pity that he should have gone off in such a hurry, just when life was opening up such happy vistas before him, vistas no longer patrolled by governesses and maid servants, nor hedged in by petty restrictions. Cosmo John had died one hundred years ago, in May—and, by the Rood! this was May! Had he ever been a-fishing. Had the sudden tremor of the rod made his young heart to leap? I heard the Bishop's rich voice roll on:

"—Most heartily we beseech Thee with Thy favour to behold our most gracious Sovereign Lady, Queen Victoria; and so replenish her with the grace of Thy Holy Spirit that she may alway incline to Thy will"—the Bishop's voice became one with the murmur of the river, as it moved among the ridges; the mellow sunlight scarcely touched this sheltered pool, but one could see it in its full strength on the meadow beyond, where larks were nesting. I brought myself up with a start. The Bishop's voice came from a great distance—"beseech Thee to bless Albert Edward Prince of Wales"—Angel was joggling me with his elbow.

"You duffer," he whispered, "you've been nodding. Get your hymn book."

In the choir vestry the Bishop stopped for a moment beside us, his surplice billowing about him like the sails about a tall mast when the wind dies. "At seven," he said, "tomorrow morning at my house. And wear old clothes."

The sails were filled, and he moved majestically away, towering above the small craft around him.

II

It was morning. It was ten o'clock. It was May. We were all stowed away in the Bishop's trap with his son, Harry, controlling the fat pony, whose small fore-hoof pawed impatiently on the asphalt. Angel and I had donned old jerseys and The Seraph a clean holland pinafore, against which he pressed an empty treacle tin where a solitary worm reared an anxious head against the encircling gloom.

"I've got a worm," he gasped, gleefully, as the pony, released at last, jerked us almost off our seats. "He's nice an' fat, an' he's quite clean, for I've washed him fwee times. He's as tame as anyfing. He's wather a dear ole worm, an' it seems a shame to wun a hook frew him."

"Child, it shall not be done," consoled the Bishop. "Keep your worm, and, when we get to the river-bank, we'll introduce him to the country worms, and maybe he'll like them so well he'll marry and settle down there for the rest of his days."

"If he could see a lady-worm he'd like," stipulated The Seraph.

"He'd have a wide choice," said the Bishop. "The country is full of worms, some of them charming, I daresay."

"And, I say," chuckled Angel, "you could perform the ceremony—if only we knew their names."

"This is Charles Augustus," said The Seraph with dignity.

"She'd likely be Ernestine," I put in.

"Very well," said the Bishop. "It should proceed thus: 'I, Charles Augustus, take thee, Ernestine, to have and to hold'—and I do wish, Harry, that you'd have a care and hold Merrylegs in. He's almost taking our breath away. Such a speed is undignified, and bad for the digestion."

It was true that the fat pony was in amazing spirits that morning. Shops and houses were passed with exhilarating speed. To us little fellows, who always walked with our governess, when we went abroad, it was intoxicating.

Soon the town was left behind and we were bowling along a country road past a field where boys were flying a kite, its long tail making sinuous curves against the turquoise sky. The air was sweet with the fresh May showers; and the swift roll of wheels was an inspiring accompaniment to our chatter.

Further along lay a tranquil pond in a common, its surface stirred by a tiny boat with white sails. An old, white-bearded man in a smock frock was teaching his grandsons to sail the boat. It must be jolly, we thought, to have a nice old grandfather to play with one.

At last we passed a vine-embowered inn, set among apple trees in bloom. It was "The Sleepy Angler" and the Bishop said that the river curved just beyond it.

We gave a shout of joy as we caught the glint of it; a shout that might well have been a warning to any lurking trout. Angel and I scarcely waited for the pony to draw up beneath the trees before we tumbled out of the trap; and the Bishop, grasping the eager Seraph by the wrist, swung him to the ground after us.

We felt very small and light, and almost fairy-like, as we ran here and thither over the lush grass, studded with spring flowers. Our sensitive nostrils were greeted by enticing new odors that seemed to be pressed from the springy sod of our scampering feet. The Seraph still clutched the treacle tin, and Charles Augustus must have had a bad quarter hour of it.

The stream, which was a sharp, clear one, sped through flowery meadows, where geese were grazing as soberly as cows. An old orchard enfolded it, at last, scattering pink petals on its flowing cloud-flecked surface, and drawing new life from its freshness.

Harry made the pony comfortable and lit his pipe, and the Bishop got ready his tackle, while the three of us clustered about him, filled with wonder and delight to see the book of many coloured flies, and all the intricacies of preparing the rod and bait. Angel and I were equipped with proper rods baited with greenish May-flies, and The Seraph got a willow wand and line at the end of which dangled an active grasshopper.

"You know," said the Bishop, when we had cast our flies, "if I were a whole-hearted angler, I should not have brought three such restless spirits on this expedition but truly I am—

    'No fisher,
    But a well-wisher
    To the game!'

So, now that you are here, suppose I give you a lesson in manipulating your tackling. If you proceed as you have begun, there will very soon not be so much as a minnow within a mile of us. Easy now, Angel; just move your fly gently on top of the water so that his bright wings may attract the eye of the most wanton trout. Easy, John—by the lord, I've caught a Greyling! And come and sniff him, and you'll find he smells of water-thyme."

How aptly we took to this sort of teaching, given in the fresh outdoors, the air pleasant with honeysuckle, and a lark carolling high above us! We could scarcely restrain our shouts when Angel's first trout was landed with the aid of a net, and lay golden and white as a daffodil on the grass. So absorbed were we that no one gave any heed to The Seraph, stationed farther down stream, till a roar of

111

rage discovered him, dancing empty-handed on the bank, his rod sailing smartly down the stream, leaving only a wake of tiny ripples.

"It was a 'normous lusty trout," he wailed, "as big as a whale, an' he swallowed my grasshopper, an' hook, an' gave me such a look! And I'd pwomised him to Mary Ellen for her tea!"

"We may as well give up for a while," said the Bishop, mildly, "and have some lunch. Bring The Seraph to me, boys, and I shall comfort him, whilst you unpack the hamper."

What hearty, wholesome appetites we brought to the cold beef and radishes! And how much more satisfying such fare than the milky messes served to us by Mrs. Handsomebody! Harry had buried a bottle of ale under the cool sod, and we had tastes of that to wash our victuals down. Even Charles Augustus had a little of it poured into his cell to comfort him.

When we were satisfied, the Bishop retired to the shade of a hedge with his pipe; The Seraph wandered off by himself to hunt for birds' nests; and Angel and I took fresh flies and tried our luck anew. But the sun was high; the south breeze was fallen; and the trout had sought their farthest chambers in the pool.

Angel soon tired when sport flagged.

"Let's go find the kid," he said, throwing down the rod, "he'll be getting himself drowned if we don't keep an eye on him. I'll race you to that nearest apple tree!"

With nimble legs, and swiftly beating hearts, we scampered over the smooth turf, and I threw a triumphant look over my shoulder at him, as I hurled myself upon the mossy bole of the old tree. Then I saw that Angel had stopped stock still and was staring open-mouthed beyond me. I turned. Then, I, too, stared open-mouthed. Trust The Seraph for falling on his feet! What though his rod had been filched—here he was, without a moment's loss, plunged in a new adventure!

III

He was seated beneath an apple tree, on the bank of the stream in deep conversation with a most remarkable old man, who was fishing industriously with the very rod The Seraph so lately had bewailed. He was an astonishingly old man, with hair and beard as white as wool, wreathing a face as pink as the apple-blossoms that fell about him. Cautiously we drew near, quite unobserved by the two who seemed utterly absorbed in their occupation of watching the line as it dipped into the stream. Now we could see that the old man's clothes were ragged, and that he had taken off his boots to ease his tired feet, the toes of which protruded from his socks, even pinker than his face.

He was speaking in a full soft voice with an accent which was new to us.

"Yon trout," said he, "was in a terrible frizz wi' the hook gnawing his vitals, and he swum about among the reeds near the bank in a manner to harrer your feelings. The line got tangled in the growing stuff, and I, so quick as an otter, pounced on him, and had him on the bank afore 'ee could say 'scat,' and there he lies breathing his last, and blessing me no doubt for relieving him in his shameful state."

"I fink he's weally my twout," said The Seraph. "I caught him first you see."

"That pint might take a terr'ble understanding lawyer to unravel," replied the old man, "but sooner than quarrel in such an unsporting fashion, I'll give 'ee the trout, though I had had a notion of roasting him to my own breakfast."

The Seraph stroked the glistening side of the recumbent trout admiringly; he poked his plump forefinger into it's quivering pink gill. The result was startling. The trout leaped into the air with a flourish of silvery tail; then fell floundering on The Seraph's bare knees. Our junior, seized with one of his unaccountable impulses, grasped him by the middle and hurled him into the stream. A second more and the trout was gone, leaving only a thin line of red to mark his passing. Angel and I ran forward to protect The Seraph if need be from the consequences of his hardy act; but the old man was smiling placidly.

"That trout," he said, "is so gleeful to get away from his captivity as I be to escape from the work'us."

"Oh, did you run away from the workhouse?" we cried, in chorus,

113

gathering around him, "Have you run far?" And we looked at his broken boots.

"I ban't a dareful man," he replied, "that would run down the road in daylight for the whole nation to see, and I be terr'ble weak in the legs, so I just crept out in the night, so quiet as a star-beam, and sheltered in the orchard yonder, till I seed the rod fairly put in my hand by the Almighty, that I mid strike manna out of the stream, like old Moses, so to speak."

"You're a funny man," said Angel. "You've a rum way of talking."

"I come from Devon by natur," he answered, "and my tongue still has the twist o't though I haven't seed the moors these sixty years."

"You must be pretty old."

"Old! I be so aged that I can remember my grandmother when she was but a rosy-cheeked slip of a gal."

We stared in awe before such antiquity.

The Seraph ventured: "Did your grandmother put you in the work'us?"

"No, no. Not she. It was my two grandsons. Well-fixed men they be too, for Philip had a fine cow until the bailiff took her; and Zachary thinks naught on a Fair day o' buying meat pasties for hisself and his missus, and parading about before the nation wi' the gravy fair running down their wrists. Ay—but the work'us was good enough for old Granfa. 'Darn'ee,' says I to Philip, 'there's life in the old dog yet, and I'll escape from here in the fulness of time!' Which I did."

We grouped ourselves about him in easy attitudes of attention. We felt strangely drawn to this ancient rebel against authority. We pictured the workhouse as a vast schoolroom where white-haired paupers laboured over impossible tasks, superintended by a matron, cold and angular, like Mrs. Handsomebody.

"Are your own children all dead?" I put the question timidly, for I feared to recall more filial ingratitude.

"Dead as door-nails," he replied, solemnly. "All of them."

"Were there many?"

"When I had been married but seven years, there were six; and after that I lost count. At that time I was moved to compose a little song about them, and I'd sing it to 'ee this moment if I had a bite o' victuals to stay me."

"Look here, Seraph," I cried, "You cut back to the hamper and fetch some beef and bread, and anything else that's loose. Look sharp, now."

The Seraph ran off obediently, and it was not long till he reappeared with food and the dregs of the ale.

It was a treat to see Granfa make way with these. He smacked his lips and wiped his beard on his sleeve with the relish born of prolonged abstinence. As he ate, the apple-blossoms fell about him, settling on the rim of his ragged hat, and even finding shelter among the white waves of his beard. We sat cross-legged on the grass before him eagerly awaiting the song.

At last, in a voice rich with emotion, he sang to a strange lilting tune:

"I be in a terr'ble fix,
Wife have I and childer six.

"I'd got married just for fun,
When in popped Baby Number one—

"I'd got an easy job to do,
When in strolled Baby Number Two—

"I was fishin' in the sea,
When up swum Baby Number Three—

"My boat had scarcely touched the shore,
When in clumb Baby Number Four!

"I was the scaredest man alive,
When wife found Baby Number Five.

"The cradle was all broke to sticks
When in blew Baby Number Six—

"And now I'm praying hard that Heaven
Will keep a grip on Number Seven."

"And did Heaven keep a gwip on it?" inquired The Seraph as soon as the last notes died away.

"Not a bit of it," responded our friend. "They come along so fast that I was all in a mizmaze trying to keep track on 'em. And good childer they was, and would never have turned me out as their sons have had the stinkin' impidence to do. But now, souls, tell me all about yourselves, for I be a terr'ble perusin' man and I like to ponder on the doings of my fellow-creatures. Did you mention the name of a parson, over by yon honeysuckle hedge?"

We thought the old man was excellent; and we found it an easy thing to make a confidant of him. So, while he puffed at a stubby clay pipe, we drew closer and told him all about the Bishop and about father and how lonely we were for him. Blue smoke from his clay pipe spun about us, seeming to bind us lightly in a fine web of friendship. Through it his blue eyes shone longingly, his pink face shone with sympathy, and his white beard with its clinging apple-blossom petals, rose and fell on his ragged breast.

"It's a great pity," said Angel, "that father isn't here now, because I'm certain he'd be jolly glad to adopt you for a grandfather for us. He's a most reasonable man."

Our new friend shook his head doubtfully.

"It would be a noble calling," he said, "but I ban't wanted by nobody I'm afeard. I think I'll just bide here by this pleasant stream, till in the fulness of time I be food for worms."

"Could Charles Augustus have a little of you?" asked The Seraph, sweetly.

"Ess Fay, he may have his share." It appeared that the story of Charles had been told before Angel and I had arrived.

"Well, you're not going to be deserted," said Angel, in his lordly way, "we'll just adopt you on our own. Mrs. Handsomebody won't let us have a dog, nor a guinea pig, nor rabbits, nor even a white rat, but, you bet, she's got to let us keep a grandfather, if we take him right home and say he's come for a visit, and, of course, father'll have to pay for his board. Let's do it, eh John?"

When Angel's eyes sparkled with a conquering light, few could resist him. Certainly not I, his faithful adherent. Anyway I wanted Granfa myself badly, so I nodded solemnly. "Let's."

116

"It'll be the greatest lark ever," he said, "and here comes the Bishop."

"Hand me my shoon, quick," said Granfa, nervously.

The Bishop was indeed coming slowly toward us, across the sun-lit meadow, carrying his rod in one hand, and in the other the tin containing Charles Augustus. By the time he had reached us Granfa had struggled into his boots and was standing, hat in hand, with an air of meek expectancy. Angel, always so fluent when we were by ourselves, balked at explaining things to grown-ups, and, though the Bishop usually saw things from our point of view, one could never be absolutely certain that even he would not prove obtuse on such a delicate issue as this.

So I rose, and met his enquiring look with such explanation as suited his adult understanding.

"Please, sir," I said, politely, "this nice old man has been turned out by his grandsons, and he's on his way to town, where he's got some kind grandsons—"

—"Fwee of 'em," put in The Seraph.

—"And we were wondering," I hurried on, "if you'd give him a lift that far."

"I expect you're tired out," said the Bishop, kindly, turning to Granfa.

"I be none too peart, but terrible wishful to get under the roof o' my grandsons, thank 'ee."

"You shall have a seat beside Harry; I see you've had some lunch; and now, boys, I think we have time for an hour's fishing before we go, but first we must dispose of Charles Augustus. I don't like the way he looks. I don't know whether he's just foxy and pretending he's dead so we shan't use him for bait, or whether the ale was too much for him. At any rate, he's looking far from well." And the Bishop peered anxiously into the treacle tin.

So the search began for the ideal mate for Charles Augustus. He was laid in state on a large burdock leaf, where he stretched himself warily enough in the fervent heat of the sun. The Seraph, quick as a robin, was the first to pounce upon a large, but active dew-worm, which, he announced, was Ernestine.

117

We made an excited little group around the burdock, as The Seraph, flushed with pride, deposited her beside the lonely Charles. She glided toward him. She touched him. The effect was electrical. Charles Augustus, after one violent contortion, hurled himself from the burdock, and, before we could intercept him, disappeared into a bristling forest of grass blades.

"He's gone! He's gone!" wailed The Seraph. "He's wun away fwom her!"

But, even as he spoke, the agile Ernestine leapt lightly from the trembling leaf in hot pursuit. Green spears bent to open a way for her; dizzy gnats paused in their droning song, feeling in the ether the tremor of the chase; bees fell from the heart of honey-sweet flowers, and lay murmuring and booming in the grass.

They were gone. An ant had mounted the burdock leaf, and, careless of the drama that had just been enacted, sought eagerly among the crevices for provender. The Bishop spoke first.

"I think she'll get him," he said musingly. "She's got a sort of cave-woman look, and she has no petticoats to impede her."

"Ess fay," assented Granfa, "her'll get him, and hold him fast too, I'll be bound. A terr'ble powerful worm."

We stood in silence for a space, our eyes fixed on the ground picturing that chase through dim subterranean passages, smelling of spring showers; Charles Augustus, wasted, febrile, panting with agitation; Ernestine, lithe, ardent, awful in her purpose.

We were still pensive when we retraced our steps across the meadow. The Bishop and Harry and The Seraph resumed their fishing, but Angel and I preferred to be on the grass beside Granfa, while he told us tales of old smuggling days in Devon and Cornwall, where his little cutter had slipped round about the delicate yet rugged coast, loaded with brandy and bales of silk from France, guided by strange red and blue lights from the shore; and where solemn cormorants kept darkly secret all they saw when they sailed aloft at dawn.

IV

We were delighted with Granfa. It seemed to us that the acquiring of him was the finest thing we had yet done. This elation of spirit remained with us during all the drive home. The grey old town was wrapped in a golden mist of romance; its windows reflected the fire of the sunset. It was not until we had separated from the Bishop and stood, a group of four, before Mrs. Handsomebody's house, that dread misgiving took the pith out of our legs. All of a sudden Granfa loomed bulky and solid; the problem of where he was to be stowed presented itself. He was not like Giftie to be hidden in the scullery. He was not even like a white rat that could be secreted under one's bed till its unfortunate odour resulted in painful research. No; Granfa must be accounted for, and that soon.

"Better go round to the back," suggested Angel, "and tackle Mary Ellen first."

So we traversed the chill passage between the tall houses, and softly lifted the latch of the kitchen door. Mary Ellen was alone, her work done, her nose buried in a novel of such fine print that it necessitated the lamp's being perilously near the fringe of frowsy hair that covered her forehead. We were inside the kitchen before she was recalled from the high life in which she revelled.

"Is it yersilves?" she exclaimed, with a start. "Sure, you've give me a nice fright prowlin' about like thaves—and whoiver may be the ould man wid ye? The mistress'll stand no tramps or beggars about, as well you know."

"He's no tramp or beggar," I retorted, stoutly, "he's Granfa."

"Granfa! Granfa who? Noan o' your nonsense, now, byes. What's the truth now, spit it out!"

"He's Granfa," I reiterated, desperately, "Our own nice grandfather that we haven't seen for years, and—he's just come for a nice little visit with us. Why, Mary Ellen, the Bishop knows him—"

"Known him for years," put in Angel. "Went to Harrow together."

"Ess fay," assented Granfa, eagerly. "Us were boon companions up to Harrer."

119

"The Bishop brought him wight here in the pony twap," added The Seraph, "and we'd all yike a little nushment, please."

Mary Ellen, in spite of herself, was half convinced. Granfa's blue eyes were so candid; there was an air of dignity about his snow-white locks and beard, that disarmed hostility.

"Look here, now," said Mary Ellen, in an aside, to us, "he seems a nice ould gentlemin enough, but think av the throuble ye got us in over Giftie, sure I won't have yez experimentalling wid grandfathers."

Granfa appeared to have overheard, for he spoke up.

"I just want to bide here a little while, my dearie, till I hear from my son in South Americer. The other two put me out, you see, so I've only him to depend on, till I be called away."

Mary Ellen flushed. "You'd be welcome to stay if it was my house, sir; but my misthress is to be reckoned wid. By God's mercy, she is off to a missionary meeting tonight, her bein' president av the society for makin' Unitarians out av the blacks. Sorra a thing will she hear of this till mornin', and I'll put you in my own bed, and slape on two cheers in the scullery, for it'd niver do for the boys' grandfather to be used like a beggar-man."

We thought it a capital idea for Mary Ellen to sleep in the scullery— it would save her the fag of running downstairs in the morning to get breakfast, and Granfa would be conveniently placed for us, in case we wanted a story or game before breakfast.

So, after partaking of a little nourishment, as The Seraph put it, we retired to Mary Ellen's room; she leading the way up the dark backstairs with a lighted candle; Granfa next bearing his little bundle; and we three in the rear, exceedingly tired, but in excellent spirits.

Granfa looked very snug in Mary Ellen's bed, with his curly beard resting comfortably on the red and white quilt, and his blue eyes twinkling up at us.

"Comfy, Granfa?" asked The Seraph.

"I be just so cozy as an old toad," he replied. "I do believe I'm a-going to be terr'ble happy in my new home."

120

Mary Ellen had gone downstairs to prepare her place in the scullery, so we climbed on the bed with him, making believe it was a smuggler's cutter, and had many hair-raising adventures that were brought to an end, at last, by the discovery that Granfa was fast asleep.

We were at the windlass heaving up the anchor, at the time, and had just struck up a sailor's chanty, which made a good deal of noise, but nothing seemed to disturb Granfa. He slumbered peacefuly through all the rattle of chains, and shouting of commands, so, somewhat subdued, we decided there was nothing for it but to seek our berths.

Snug beneath our covers, at last, we felt to the full, the new spirit of adventure that had spread its irridescent wings over the house. There was Granfa, snoring under Mary Ellen's patchwork quilt; there was the trusty Mary Ellen, herself, stowed away in the scullery; there was Mrs. Handsomebody, on missionary duty among the blacks; here were we—The Seraph expressed our feelings exactly just before we fell asleep. "We'm terr'ble lucky chaps," he said, in the Devon dialect, "ban't us?"

V

Our bedroom window was always tightly closed, and, at night, so were the shutters; yet a sunbeam, adventurous, like ourselves, found its way through a broken slat, and, cleaving the heavy air of the chamber, flew straight to The Seraph's nose, where it perched, lending a radiant prominence to that soft feature.

The Seraph roused himself. He opened his eyes; the sunbeam found them two dark forest pools, and plunged therein. The Seraph opened his mouth and laughed, showing all his little white teeth, and the sunbeam dived straightway down his throat.

"Hurrah!" cried The Seraph, "let's get up!" And scrambled out of bed.

At the same instant came a loud tapping on the door of Mary Ellen's bedroom. We surmised, correctly, that Mrs. Handsomebody, listening in vain for the sound of her handmaiden's descent of the back stairs had risen wrathfully, and come to summon her in person. A chill of apprehension ran along my spine. I got up and

121

stole to the door, followed by my brothers. Through a crack we peered fearfully in the direction of the rapping, our trembling bodies close together.

Mrs. Handsomebody, in purple dressing-gown and red woollen slippers, stood in a listening attitude, her gaze bent on the door that hid Granfa.

"Are you aware of the hour?" she demanded peremptorily. "Rise at once and open this door."

There was a creaking of the mattress and sound of shuffling feet; the door was opened reluctantly, and Granfa, bare-legged, white of beard and red-shirted, stood in the aperture.

Mrs. Handsomebody did not shriek; rather she made the inarticulate noises of one in a nightmare and put out her hands as if to keep Granfa off. "Merciful Heaven!" she whispered. "What has happened to you?"

"I do feel far from peart," replied Granfa.

"This is horrible. Did you feel it coming on?"

"Off and on for a long time," said Granfa. "It's been a terr'ble experience, and I ban't likely to be ever the same again, I'm afeared."

Mrs. Handsomebody looked ready to faint.

At that moment, Mary Ellen, having heard the voice of her mistress, projected her face above the doorsill of the backstairs. It was always a rosy face, but now with excitement and shamefacedness, it was as red as a harvest moon, coming up from the darkness.

The sight of her turned Mrs. Handsomebody's terror into rage.

"Shameful, depraved girl," she gobbled, "who is this you have in your chamber? Ah, I've caught you! The ingratitude! You terrible old wretch!"—this to Granfa—"close that door instantly while I send for the police!"

By this time we had ventured into the hall, and, Mrs. Handsomebody, seeing us groaned: "Under the roof with these innocent children—I thought that in my care their innocence was safe."

122

"It was thim same innocents that brung him here," said Mary Ellen, stung into disclosing our part in the scandal, "and it's himsilf is their own grandfather."

Mrs. Handsomebody's gaze was appalling as she turned it on us three.

"You? Your grandfather? What fresh insanity is this?"

"You see," I explained, keeping my fascinated eyes on the wart on her chin, "he's just come for a little visit, and he really is our Granfa, and we love him awfully."

"Won't have him abused," spluttered The Seraph.

"Be rights," added Mary Ellen, solemnly, "he should have the best spare room, the byes' own aged relation."

"I shall sift this affair," said Mrs. Handsomebody, "to its most appalling dregs. You, Alexander"—to The Seraph—"are the smallest, look through that keyhole and inform me what he is doing."

The Seraph obeyed, chuckling. "He's took to the bed again—all exceptin' one leg—"

"We can dispense with detail," cut in our governess. "Is he at all violent?"

"Bless you, no," replied Mary Ellen. "He's as mild mannered as can be and an old friend of the Bishop's, so they say. 'Twas him that brung him home in his pony trap."

"The Bishop! I must see the Bishop instantly."

As she spoke a stentorian shout of "Butcher!" came from the regions below.

"There," she said, to Mary Ellen, "is young Watlin. Call him up instantly; and he shall guard the door while I dress. Explain the situation very briefly to him. It would be well to arm him with a poker, in case the old man becomes violent. David, go to Bishop Torrance and tell him that I hope he will call on me at once, if possible. Put on your clothes, but you may leave your hair in disorder, just as it is. It will serve to show the Bishop into what a state of panic this household has been thrown."

123

She was obliged to retire hastily to her room because of the arrival of Mr. Watlin.

It was some time before Mary Ellen, and The Seraph, and I could make him understand what had happened, though we all tried at once.

"And you mean to tell me that he's in there?" he asked, at last, grinning broadly.

"Sorra a place else," replied Mary Ellen, "and you're to guard the door till the police comes."

"Guard nothink," said Mr. Watlin, belligerently, "I'll go right in and tackle him single-handed."

With one accord The Seraph and I flung ourselves before the door.

"You shan't hurt him," we cried, "he's our own Granfa! We'll fight you first."

Mr. Watlin made some playful passes at our stomachs. "Let's all have a fight," he chaffed. Then he said—"Hullo, here's the old 'un himself, and quite a character to be sure. No wonder Mrs. 'Andsomebody is in a taking."

The door had opened behind us; Granfa stood revealed, wearing his ragged coat and hat, and carrying his stick and little bundle, wrapped in a red handkerchief.

"Don't 'ee get in a frizz, my dears, about me," he said with dignity. "I be leaving this instant moment. As for you—" addressing Mr. Watlin—"you be a gert beefy critter, but don't be too sure you could tackle me, single-handed. I be terr'ble full of power when I'm roused, and it takes a deal to calm me down again." And he trotted to the head of the stairs and began to descend.

The Seraph and I kept close on either side of him, tightly holding his hands.

"She's in the parlour," I whispered, "and the Bishop's with her. Shall you go in?"

Granfa nodded solemnly.

We stood in the doorway of the sacred apartment. Even there, the spirit of the May morning seemed to have penetrated, for in the glass case a stuffed oriole had cocked his eye with a longing look at a withered nest that hung before him.

Mrs. Handsomebody had just finished her recital. "I thought I should have swooned," she said.

"And no wonder," replied the Bishop, "I'm quite sure I should have." Then he turned to us with a look of mingled amusement and concern. "Now what do you suppose I'm going to do with you Granfa?"

"Oh, parson, don't 'ee send me back to the work'us! If I bide there any longer, 'twill break my fine spirit."

"I am going to propose something very different," said the Bishop, kindly. "We need another sweeper and duster about the Cathedral, and if you think you are strong enough to wield a broom, you may earn a decent living. I know a very kind charwoman, who would lodge and board you, and you would be near your little—"

"Gwandsons," said The Seraph.

"Silence!" ordered Mrs. Handsomebody.

"You would be near us all," finished the Bishop, blandly.

"Ess fay. I can wield a broom," said Granfa. "And 'twill be a noble end for me to pass my days in such a holy spot. 'Twill be but a short jump from there fair into Heaven itself, and I do thank 'ee, parson, with all my heart."

So it was settled, and turned out excellently. Even Mary Ellen could have learned from Granfa new ways of handling a broom with the least exertion to the worker; aye, in his hands, the broom seemed used chiefly as a support; a staff, upon which he leant while telling us many a tale of those rare old smuggling days of his youth.

Sometimes, in dim unused parts of the building, we would rig up a pirate's ship, and Granfa would fix the broom to the masthead to show that he, like Drake, had swept the seas.

Sometimes, indeed, we found him fast asleep in a corner of some crimson-cushioned pew, looking so peaceful that, rough sea-going fellows though we were, we had not the heart to rouse him.

125

Once, standing before the stained glass window in memory of young Cosmo John, Granfa said:

"It beats all how thiccy lad does yearn toward me. His eyes follow me wherever I go."

"And no wonder, Granfa," cried The Seraph, throwing his arms around him, "for everybody loves 'ee so!"

Chapter VIII

Noblesse Oblige

I

Angel and I grew amazingly that summer. We grew in length of limb but with no corresponding gain in scholastic stature. We had made up our minds to retain as little as possible of Mrs. Handsomebody's teaching and we had succeeded so well in our purpose, that, at nine and ten we had about as much book-learning as would have befitted The Seraph, while he retained the serene ignorance of babyhood. But in affairs of the imagination we were no laggards. We eagerly drank in Granfa's tales of the sea, and Harry lent us many a hair-raising book of adventure.

Yet we longed for the companionship of other boys of our own age, and strained towards the day when we should go to school. Our abounding energy chafed more and more under the rule of Mrs. Handsomebody.

Now she had left the schoolroom to interview a plumber, and her black bombazine dress having sailed away like a cloud, we had utterly relaxed, and were basking in the sunshine of her absence.

Slumped on my spine, I was watching a spider, just over my head, that was leisurely ascending his shining rope-ladder to the ceiling. I contemplated his powers of retreat with an almost bitter envy. Fancy being able, at a moment's notice, to bolt out of reach (even out of sight and hearing) of all that was obnoxious to a fellow! I pictured myself, when some particularly harassing question had been put by my governess, springing from my seat, snatching the ever-ready shining rope and making for some friendly cornice, where, with my six or eight legs wrapped round my head, I would settle down for a snug sleep, not to be disturbed by any female.

Yet, I had to admit, that if any one in the schoolroom played the rôle of spider, it was Mrs. Handsomebody herself, whose desk was the centre of a web of books, pencils, rulers and a cane, in the meshes of which we three were caught like young flies, before our bright wings had been unfolded.

127

I looked at The Seraph. After slavishly making pot hooks all the afternoon, he was now licking them off his slate with unaffected relish. I turned to Angel.

With hands thrust deep in his pockets he was staring disconsolately at the unfinished sum before him. I, too, had given it up in despair.

"It's mediocre," he muttered. "Absolutely mediocre, and I won't stand it."

Mediocre. It was a new word to me, and I wondered where he had picked it up. It was like Angel to spring it on me this way.

"Awfully mediocre," I assented. "And it can't be done."

A flicker of annoyance crossed his face that his new word should be thus lightly bandied, but he went on—"Just listen here: an apple-woman who had four score of apples in her cart, sold three dozen at four pence, half-penny a dozen; two and a half dozen at five pence a dozen. At what price would she have to sell the remaining, in order to realize"—

"And look here," I interrupted, wrathfully, "Why does she always give us sums about an apple-woman, or a muffin-man? It just makes a chap hungry. Why doesn't she make one up about a dentist for a change, or somethin' like that?"

"Yes," assented Angel, catching at the idea. "Like this: if a dentist pulled five teeth out of one lady, and seven and a half out of another, at two shillings apiece how many must he pull in order to—"

"Then there's undertakers," I broke in. "If a undertaker buried nine corpses one day, and six and a half the next—"

I had to stop, for Angel was convulsed with laughter, and The Seraph was beginning to get noisy.

Angel produced a small bottle of licorice water from his pocket and took a long mouthful. Then he handed it to me. It was soothing, delicious.

"Me too!" cried The Seraph, and I held it to his eager little mouth.

"Here," said Angel angrily, "he's swiggin' down the whole thing. Drop it, young'un!"

At the same moment, the door opened quietly, and Mrs. Handsomebody entered. I tore the bottle from The Seraph's clinging lips, and stuffed it, corkless, into my pocket.

Mrs. Handsomebody sat down and disposed her skirt about her knees. Her eyes travelled over us.

"Alexander," she said to The Seraph, "stand up." He meekly rose.

"What is that on your chin?"

The Seraph explored his chin with his tongue.

"It tastes sweet," he said.

"I asked what is it?"

The Seraph shot an imploring glance at Angel.

"I fink," he hedged, "it's some of the gwavy fwom dinner left over."

Mrs. Handsomebody turned to Angel and me.

"Stand up," she commanded, sternly, "and we shall sift this matter to the root."

"Yes," admitted Angel, nonchalantly. "It was licorice root made into a drink."

"Licorice root," repeated our governess, in a tone of disgust. "It is by imbibing such vile concoctions that the taste for more ardent spirits is created. When I was your age, I had taken no beverage save milk and hot water, from which I graduated naturally to weak tea, and from thence to the—er—stronger brew. I am at present your guardian as well as your teacher and I shall do my utmost to eradicate—"

It was impossible to follow her discourse because of the keen discomfort I was feeling as the remainder of the licorice water trickled down my right leg. I was brought up with a start by Mrs. Handsomebody almost shouting:

"John! What is that puddle on the floor beneath you? Don't move! Stay where you are." She sprang to my side and grasped my shoulder.

"I s'pose it's some more of the woot," giggled The Seraph.

129

I put my hand in my pocket and produced the empty bottle. Mrs. Handsomebody took it between her thumb and forefinger. She gave me a sharp rap on the head with it.

"Now," she gobbled, "go to your room and remain there till the exercises are over, then return to me for punishment. And change your trousers."

II

My trousers had been changed. Afternoon school was over, and I had just finished the last weary line in the long imposition set by Mrs. Handsomebody. I stretched my cramped limbs, and wondered dully where my brothers were. My depression was increased by the fact that the freshly-donned trousers were brown tweed, while my jacket was of blue serge.

I laid the imposition on Mrs. Handsomebody's desk, and listlessly set out to find the others. I could hear Mary Ellen in the kitchen thumping a mop against the legs of the furniture in a savage manner that bespoke no mood of airy persiflage. Therefore, I did not go down the back stairs, but throwing a leg over the hand-rail of the front stairs, I slowly slid to the bottom, and rested there a space on my stomach, an attitude peaceful, and conducive to clear thinking.

I reviewed the situation dispassionately. Here was I, who had scarcely been at all to blame, humiliated, an outcast, so to speak, while Angel, who had made the beastly mess, went unscathed. As for The Seraph! I could scarcely bear to think of him with his tell-tale sticky little chin.

Voices roused me. Buoyant with animation, they penetrated beyond the closed front door. A loud unknown voice, mingled with those of Angel and The Seraph.

In an instant, I was on my feet, my nose pressed against one of the narrow windows of ruby-coloured glass that were on either side of the hall door. I could see three small red figures in animated conversation on the square grass plot before the house. The largest of the three began to execute a masterly hop, skip and jump on the crimson grass. Above arched the sanguine sky.

130

I opened the door and closing it softly behind me, stood on the steps.

The newcomer was a sturdy fellow about a year older than Angel. He had a devil-may-care air about him, and he wore, at a rakish angle, a cap, bearing the badge of a well-known school. He turned to me instantly.

"Well," he said, "you're a rum-lookin' pup."

I was rather abashed at such a greeting, but I held my ground. "My name is John," I replied simply.

"Oh, Lord!" he groaned. "John! Don't you know enough to give your surname? Eh? I wish we had you at my school for a term. We'd lick you into shape."

"His surname is Curzon, too," put in Angel, "same as mine."

"Very well, then," said the boy, "you're Curzon major, Curzon minor, and Curzon minimus. Hear that, Curzon minimus?" he shouted, tweaking The Seraph's ear.

"I say," said Angel, "you let him alone!" And I ran down the steps. The boy stared.

"Don't you keep him in order?" he asked.

"Rather," replied Angel, "but I don't hurt him for nothing."

"I have two young brothers," said the boy, "and I hurt them for next to nothing. Licks 'em into shape."

He looked around him and then added, "There's no fun here. Let's hook it to my place, and I'll show you my rabbits. I've taken a fancy to you, and, if you like, I'll let you call me by my first name. It's Simon. And I'll call you by yours. That minor and minimus business is rather rotten when you're friends. Come along."

Mrs. Handsomebody, we knew, was safe at a lecture on The Application of Science to Human Relationships; Mary Ellen was doing her Friday's cleaning; therefore, we set off with our new-found friend without fear of hindrance from the female section of our household.

131

As we trotted along, Simon told us that his family had taken a large old house that had stood vacant ever since we had come to live with Mrs. Handsomebody. How often we had timidly passed its dingy front, wondering what might be within its closed shutters and deep-set front door!

Now, as we approached, we saw that the sign, To Let, had been taken down; the door and shutters were wide open; and, one of the shutters, hanging at a rakish angle, much as Simon wore his cap, gave a promise of jollity and lack of restraint within.

"We shall just cut around to the back garden," announced Simon. "The kids are there, and need putting in order by the row they are making."

We passed through a low door in the wall that separated the front garden from the back. The wall was overgrown with dusty untrimmed creepers, from which a flock of sparrows flew when the door was opened.

For a moment, we could scarcely take in the scene before us; in our experience it was so unprecedented. But Simon did not seem in the least surprised.

"Hi, kids!" he yelled, "just keep that water off us, will you! Put down that hose, Mops!"

Mops was a girl a little younger than Simon. She stood in the middle of the garden, a hose in her hands, and she was absorbed in drenching two half-naked small boys and five fox terriers, who circled around her like performers in a circus ring. The noise of yelling boys and barking dogs was terrific.

"What's she doing?" we gasped.

"It's so dev'lish hot that the hose feels bully. Like to try it?"

"I wish we had got our bathing suits," said Angel.

"Never mind. I think there's a couple of pairs of trunks in the scullery, and the young 'un can have a pinafore of Mopsie's."

He led the way down some littered steps into a basement room, where a dishevelled maid was blacking boots.

"Here Playter," he ordered, "dig up some togs for a hosing, will you? And be sharp about it, there's a love."

The girl obligingly dropped her boots, and turning out the contents of a cupboard, produced some faded blue bathing trunks.

To us they seemed shamelessly inadequate, but Simon appeared satisfied. Now he hurried us to a summer-house occupied by a family of lop-eared rabbits, and here we changed into the trunks. The Seraph required some help, and when he was stripped, I could see his little heart pounding away at his ribs, for, between the exertion of keeping up to us, and not quite understanding why he was being undressed, he was very much wrought up.

"It's just fun," I reassured him. "Don't get funky."

"I'm not," he whispered, as I tied on his trunks, "but I fink it's a dangerous enterpwise."

"Time's up," yelled Simon, "get into the game!"

We leaped from the summer-house to the grass, and, refreshing it was to our bare soles. The first onslaught from the hose almost knocked my legs from under me, and, indeed, throughout the game, Mops seemed to single me out for special attention. We three had never in our lives given way to such an abandon of wildness. The Seraph yelled till he was hoarse, and, when at last Mops surrendered the hose to Simon, the orgy grew wilder still.

In the midst of it, a French window at the back of the house opened, and a lady stood on the threshold.

My senses had received only a delicate impression of pink satin, golden hair, and flashing rings, when Simon turned the hose, in full force, on the step just below her, sending a shower of drops all about her. With a scream she fled indoors, slamming the French window.

"You got her that time, all right," said Mops, grinning roguishly.

"Who is she?" I gasped.

"Oh, just mummy," replied Simon, nonchalantly.

The French window opened again. This time a young man in grey

133

tweeds appeared. I quite expected to see him greeted with a shower also, but Simon respectfully lowered the hose.

"Did you turn that hose on your mother, Simon?" asked the young man sternly.

"Just a little," answered Simon.

"Well, the next time you do it you'll get your jacket dusted, do you hear?"

"Yes, father."

The young man disappeared into the house, three of the wet dogs following him.

"Isn't Lord Simon sweet?" asked Mops, with another roguish smile at me.

"Awfully," I replied politely, "but is the lady really your mother?"

"Let's feed," interrupted Simon, throwing down the hose, "I've a rare old twist on."

I was sorry he had interrupted us, for I yearned towards Mops, and I felt that further conversation with me would be acceptable to her, but we were swept away in the stampede for food to the basement kitchens.

They seemed immense to me, and full of the jolliest servants I had ever seen. Two men-servants in livery were playing a game of cribbage at one end of a long littered table, while several laughing maid-servants hung over their shoulders. The game was suspended at our entrance, and they all turned to ask us questions and chaff us about our appearance. One of the fox terriers jumped on the table and began nosing among the saucepans. Nobody stopped him. The fat, good-natured cook busied herself in spreading bread and butter with Sultana raisins for us; the maid-servants made a great fuss over The Seraph.

In such a whirlwind did this family live that just as I was beginning to feel at ease in this extraordinary kitchen, I was rushed back to the garden to play, a somewhat solid feeling in my stomach telling me that the bread and Sultanas had arrived.

"Hurrah for stilts," screamed Mops.

134

"Just the thing," assented Simon. "Here young Bunny and Bill, fetch the stilts, and be sharp about it—hear?" and he gave them each a punch in the ribs.

Thus encouraged, Bunny and Bill scampered across the grass, the fox-terriers yelping at their heels, and, from a convenient out-house all sizes of stilts were produced.

These accomplished children could do all manner of amazing feats on the stilts; even little Bill laughed at our awkward attempts. But, after many falls, Angel and I could limp haltingly about the garden, and experienced the new joy of looking down at things instead of up.

We noticed presently that Simon was propped against the high wall that divided this garden from the next. In a moment he called to us:

"Toddle over here and see what the old girls are doing."

"Who does he mean?" I asked Mops, as we moved stiffly, side by side.

"It's the Unaquarium parson's garden," she said. "I expect they're having a tea-fight. They're always up to something fishy."

Something ominous in the words should have warned me, but I was too elated to be heedful of signs or portents. I clutched the wall, and, with a grin of amusement, gazed down at the group of ladies, who, with two gentlemen in black, were drinking tea on the lawn.

Bunny threw a green pear at the thin legs of the taller gentleman.

The gentleman shied in a most spirited fashion, slopping his tea.

Everybody turned to look in our direction.

"Duck," hissed Mops.

But it was too late to duck. Several ladies were already sweeping towards us.

Then my soul fainted within me, for the voice of the being who ruled our little universe spoke as from a dark cloud.

"David! John! Alexander!" gobbled the Voice, "are you gone mad? Come here instantly—but no—you appear to be nude—answer me— are you nude?"

135

Mops answered for us; we were too afflicted for speech.

"If you mean naket, we're not," she said, "but the dressed-up part of us is on this side."

I was conscious of murmuring voices: What a terrible little girl; indeed the whole family; as for the mother—Yes—my pupils, and, for the present, my wards—Once they even threw a dead rat over!

Then up spoke Mrs. Handsomebody. "Put on your clothes," she ordered, "and meet me at the corner. I shall be waiting."

IV

We had put on our clothes. We had met her but, good Heaven! what a Rendezvous! She, and Angel, and I were pallid with suppressed emotions, while The Seraph's face was flushed crimson. He was weeping loudly, as he followed in our wake, and walking with some difficulty, since Angel and I, in our agitation, had put his trousers on back to front.

Mrs. Handsomebody placed us in a row, on three chairs in the dining-room, and seated herself opposite to us. After removing her bonnet, and giving it to Mary Ellen to carry upstairs to the wardrobe, she said:

"If I believed that you realized the enormity of what you have done, I should write to South America to your father, and tell him that I would no longer undertake the responsibility of three boys so evilly inclined. What do you suppose my sensations were when, at the close of the lecture, the other ladies, the professor, our pastor, and myself adjourned to the garden for tea, to find you three perched, almost nude, on a wall, in such company?"

"Do you know that those people are not respectable? The man, I am told, is a rake, who attends cockfights, and the mother of those children has been seen in the garden—tight!"

"Was that the lady in pink satin?" asked Angel, showing interest for the first time.

"I daresay. One would expect to find her in pink satin."

The lecture went on, but I did not hear it; my mind dwelt insistently on thoughts of the lady in pink.

"What did she do, please?" I interrupted, thoughtlessly, at last.

"Who do?"

"The lady. When she was tight."

"So that is where your thoughts were," said Mrs. Handsomebody, angrily, "nice speculations indeed, for a little boy!"

"I should yike a little nushment, please," interrupted The Seraph in his turn.

"Not nourishment, but punishment is what you will get, young man," replied our governess, tartly. "What you three need is discipline at the hands of a strong man. We shall now go upstairs."

V

It was over. The gas was out, and we were in bed. Not snugly in bed, but smartingly; each trying to find a cool place on the sheets, and things very much bedewed by the tears of The Seraph.

"I don't care," said Angel, rather huskily. "It was worth it, I'd do it again like a shot."

"So would I," I assented. "Whatever do you s'pose they're up to now!"

And, indeed, the thought of this spirited family coloured all my dreams. As in dancing rainbows they whirled about my bed: Mops with the hose; Bunny and Bill twinkling on stilts; Simon with all the dogs at his heels; and above all, the lady in pink, presiding like a golden-haired goddess, and very "tight."

We were still in black disgrace at breakfast. Scarcely dared we raise our eyes to the cold face of Mrs. Handsomebody, lest she should read in them some yearning recollection of yesterday's misdeeds. Large spoonfuls of porridge and thin milk made unwonted gurgling noises as they hurried down our throats to our empty young stomachs.

137

When we had done, and The Seraph had offered thanks to God for this good meal, Mrs. Handsomebody marched us, like conscripts to the schoolroom, where she assigned to each of us a task to keep him busy until her return from market.

But the front door had barely closed upon her black bombazine dress, when we scampered to the head of the stairs, threw ourselves upon the hand-rail, and slid lightly to the bottom, and from there ran to find Mary Ellen in the parlour.

She was sweeping out the sombre room with such listless movements of her plump, red arms, that the moist tea-leaves on the floor scarce moved beneath the broom.

"Sure, I niver see sich a cairpet as this in all me born days," she was saying. "If I was to swape till I fell prostitute, I'd niver git it clane."

"Oh, don't bother about the work, Mary Ellen!" we cried. "Just listen to the adventure we had yesterday!"

"I listened to the hindermost part of it," she returned, "and it sounded purty lively."

"Who cares?" said Angel. "It didn't hurt a bit."

"Not a bit," assented The Seraph, cheerily. "She gets weaker evwy day, and I get stwonger."

We rushed upon Mary Ellen then with the whole story of our new friends, dwelling, especially, upon our visit below stairs, and the rollicking men and maid-servants we found there.

"They were drinking beer-and-gin," concluded Angel, "and the scullery-maid did a breakdown for us in a pair of hunting boots."

"It beats all," said Mary Ellen, leaning on her broom, "what kapes me in a dull place like this, whin there do be sich wild goin's on just around the corner like. I'd give a month's wage to see thim folks."

"Come around with me," suggested Angel, "and I'll introduce you."

"Oh, no, Masther Angel. Misther Watlin, me young man, wouldn't want me to be goin' into mixed company widout him. An it do seem a pity, too, since I have me new blue dress, for if ever I look lovely, I look lovely in blue." And she attacked the tea-leaves with a lagging broom.

138

Mrs. Handsomebody, when dinner was over, fixed us with her cold grey eye, and said:

"Since you have proved yourselves utterly untrustworthy, you shall be locked in your bedroom, during my absence this afternoon. Mary Ellen, who will be engaged in cleaning the coal cellar, has been instructed to supply you with bread and milk at four o'clock. By exemplary behaviour today, you will ensure a return to your customary privileges tomorrow."

VI

The prison door was locked. The gaoler gone.

Thus our Saturday half-holiday!

Angel and I threw ourselves, face downward, on the bed. Not so The Seraph. Folding his arms, which were almost too short to fold, he stood before the single window, gazing through its grimy glass at the brick wall opposite, as though determined to find something cheerful in the outlook.

Aeons passed.

Familiar faces began to leer at me from the pattern in the wall-paper. Angel was despondently counting out his money on the counter-pane, and trying to make three half-pennys and a penny with a hole through it, look like affluence.

Suddenly there came a rattling of hard particles on the pane. As we stared at each other in surprise, another volley followed. It was a signal, and no mistake! Already The Seraph was tapping the window in response. A moment of violent exertion passed before we could get it open. Then, thrusting out our heads we discovered Simon standing in the passage below, his upturned face wearing an anxious grin.

"Thought I'd never get you," he whispered hoarsely. "I saw the Dragon go out, so I fired a handful of gravel at every window in turn. Come on out."

"We can't. We're locked in!" we chorused dismally.

139

"I'll try to catch you if you jump," he suggested. "I would break the fall, anyway."

But the way looked long, and Simon very small.

Then: "There's a ladder," cried The Seraph, gleefully, "better twy that."

With his usual clear-sightedness, he had spied what had escaped his seniors. Our neighbour, Mr. Mortimer Pegg, had been having some paper hung, and, surely enough, the workmen had left a tall ladder propped against the wall of the house. Without a second's hesitation, Simon flung himself upon it, and with one splendid effort, hurled it from that support to the wall of Mrs. Handsomebody's house. Then, with the strength of a superman, he dragged it until it leaned just below our window, and stood gasping at its base.

"Good fellow," said Angel, and began to climb out.

"Now, you hand me The Seraph," he ordered, "and I'll attend to him."

I had some misgivings as I passed his plump, clinging little person through the window, and watched him make the perilous descent, but, in time, he reached the ground, and then I, too, stood beside the others, and the four of us scampered lightly down the street with no misgivings, and no fears.

Before the door of our own grocer, Simon made a halt.

"Must have somethin' wet," he gasped. "Ladder nearly floored me."

He took us in and treated us with princely unconcern to ginger beer and a jam puff apiece. As we sucked our beer through straws, I smiled to think of Mary Ellen, doubtless preparing bread and milk at home.

Once more we entered the garden through the creeper-hung door. We visited the rabbits, and unchained one of the fox-terriers, which had been tied up, Simon told us, as a punishment for eating part of a lace curtain. Bill appeared then and said that his mother desired us to go to her in the drawing-room, and, as it was beginning to rain, Simon agreed that it wasn't a bad idea. We might even find something to eat in there.

As we trooped past the basement window, I lingered behind the others, and peered for a space into the lawless region below. What met my gaze almost took my breath away: for there was our own Mary Ellen, who should have been at that moment cleaning the coal cellar, sitting at one end of the long table, in her new blue dress, and plumed hat, a gentleman in livery on either side of her, and on the table before her, a mug, which, without doubt, contained gin-and-beer!

I waited to see no more. Enough to know that all the world was run amuck! With a glad whoop, I sped after the others, and only drew up when I stood on the threshold of the drawing-room.

Like the servants' hall, it was a large apartment, and, like it, was bewildering in its colour and movement, to eyes accustomed to the grey decorum of Mrs. Handsomebody's establishment.

Though it was summer, there was a fire on the hearth, which played with changeful constancy on the vivid chintzes, silver candle-sticks, and many mirrors of the room, but most of all, on the golden hair and satin tea-gown of the lady in pink.

She was speaking in a loud, clear voice to Simon's father, who was leaning against the mantelpiece smoking.

"Why the devil," she was saying, "should you smoke expensive cigars? Why don't you smoke cigarettes as I do?"

She angrily puffed at one as she spoke, and threw herself back among the black and gold cushions of the divan, where she was sitting. Her fair brow cleared, however, as her glance rested on The Seraph.

"Adorable little toad!" she cried, drawing him to her side. "What is your name?"

"Alexander," replied our youngest, "but they call me The Seraph. I'm not a pampud pet."

This sent the lady into a gale of laughter. She hugged him closer and turned to me.

"And what is your name, Sobersides?" she demanded.

"John," I replied, "and my father is David Curzon, and he is an engineer in South America, but he's coming back to England some

141

day, and, I expect then we shall go to school. We just live with Mrs. Handsomebody."

As I talked, her expression changed. She leaned forward, searching my face eagerly.

"Is it possible?" she said, in a tragic voice. "Is it possible? David Curzon. His son. The very spit of him!" Abruptly she broke into gay laughter, which, somehow, I did not quite like: and turning to her husband, she said: "Do you remember Davy Curzon? He was such a silly old pet. Lor'! I'd quite forgot him!"

"Lucky Davy," said the gentleman, smiling at me.

"And he was so ridiculously poor," she went on, "I remember he ruined himself once to buy me a pair of cream-coloured ponies, and a lapis-lazuli necklace. And I daresay he's fat now!"

"He is not," I retorted stoutly. "He's thin. He's had the fever."

"Again?" she cried. "He had it when I knew him—badly too. Who did he marry?"

"A Miss Vicars," replied her husband. "Good family. A screaming beauty too. Other two boys look like her."

But the lady had now, it seemed, no interest in the other two boys. The Seraph was deposed from his place on the divan to make room for me; and the lady begged me to give her a kiss, just for old times' sake. Yet, somehow, I did not quite like it, for I felt that she was making fun of my father, the hero of my dreams.

Meanwhile, the other children, unchided, were making things lively in their own way. Mops and the boys were eating dates from a bowl and pelting each other with the stones, while a new member of the family, a seemingly sexless being in a blue sash and shoulder knots, called "Baby," galloped up and down the room with a battledore and shuttlecock.

VII

No servant announced her name. I felt no warning tremor of solid Earth beneath my feet. Yet there she was, in full equipment of bombazine dress, hard black bonnet, reticule, and umbrella, gripped like an avenging sword. Oh, that some merciful cloud might have swept us, like fair Iphigenia to the abode of the gods, and left three soft-eyed hinds in our stead!

Yet, there we were, gazing at her, spellbound: and presently she enunciated with awful distinctness:

"I am come to apologize for the intrusion of my wards upon your privacy, and to remove them instantly."

"Oh, bless you," said the lady in pink, cheerily, "three or four more don't matter to us. Won't you sit down? And children—please let the lady's things be, d'you hear?" for these intrepid children had gathered around Mrs. Handsomebody as though she were a dancing bear; and "Baby" had even pulled her umbrella from her hand substituting for it the battledore which Mrs. Handsomebody unconsciously held, with an effect of ferocious playfulness.

"I thank you," replied Mrs. Handsomebody. "I shall remain standing."

"Let me make you acquainted with my husband," pursued the lady, "he's Lord Simon de Lacey, second son of the Duke of Aberfalden. Please excuse him smokin'!"

The effect of these simple words on Mrs. Handsomebody was startling. She brandished the battledore as though to ward off the approaching Lord Simon, and repeated in a trembling voice:

"Lord Simon de Lacey—Duke of Aberfalden. Surely there is some mistake."

"I'm afraid not," said Lord Simon, shaking her hand. "In me you behold the traditional, impecunious younger son, and—"

"But it will not always be so," interrupted Lady Simon, shouting to make herself heard, "for, you see, my husband's older brother is an invalid who will never marry, so we shall inherit the dukedom and estates one day. This child—" pointing to young Simon—"is a future duke."

"He has a lovely brow," said Mrs. Handsomebody, beaming at him.

Indeed, an astounding change had come over our governess. No longer was her manner frigid; her face, so grey and hard, had

143

softened till it seemed to radiate benevolence. She beamed at Bill and Bunny playing at leap-frog before her chair; she beamed at "Baby," galloping astride of her umbrella; she beamed at Mops, trying to force a date into the mouth of a struggling fox-terrier; she even beamed at me when I caught her eye.

"I trust that your father, the Duke, keeps well," she said to Lord Simon.

"Great old boy," he replied. "Never misses a meet. Been in at the death of nearly four thousand foxes."

"Ah, blood will tell," breathed Mrs. Handsomebody.

"You see," interposed Lady Simon, "the Duke disinherited my husband when he married me. Didn't approve of the Profession. I was Miss Dulcie June, awfully well known. Photographs all over the place. Danced at the Gaiety, y'know."

"I'm sure I have heard of you," said Mrs. Handsomebody.

"Well, the Duke and I ran into each other at a dog show last week, and he was so struck with me, he asked to be introduced, and has asked us all to visit him at Falden Castle. It looks hopeful, don't it?"

"Indeed, yes. But we shall be very sorry to lose you. It is so difficult for me to find suitable companions for my wards, and your children are so—spirited. Of course, blood will tell."

"Just what I say," assented Lady Simon, "for I was a spirited girl, if ever there was one. What with late hours, and toe-dancin' and high-kickin', it's a wonder how I stood it. I think I was like that Sir Galahad chap whose 'strength was as the strength of ten'—"

"Doubtless because your art was pure, my love," put in Lord Simon, with a sly smile.

"I used to know this boy's father in those days," went on Lady Simon. "He was a lamb."

"He was also my pupil in his youth," said Mrs. Handsomebody, and the two talked on in the happiest fashion, till we took our leave, the whole family following us to the door, and "Baby" returning Mrs. Handsomebody's umbrella, and relieving her of the battledore without her having been aware of the negotiation.

So we who had expected to be haled to retribution, as criminals of the deepest dye, floated homeward in the serene light of Mrs. Handsomebody's approval.

No one spoke till the Cathedral came in view. Then Angel said:

"There's a window in the Cathedral in memory of a son of some Duke of Aberfalden. He died about a hundred years ago."

"The very same family," replied our governess, "and, I am sure, from now on, my dear boy, you will regard the window with a new reverence."

"You must have noticed," she proceeded, "the geniality and dignity that emanated from each separate member of that noble family. This is admirably expressed by the French in the saying—'Noblesse oblige'—meaning that nobility has its obligations. Repeat the phrase after me, David, that you may acquire a perfect accent."

"Knob-less obleedge," repeated Angel, submissively; and The Seraph also repeated it several times, as though storing it away for future use.

When Mrs. Handsomebody rang the door-bell, I trembled for Mary Ellen, remembering where I had last seen her, but the admirable girl promptly opened the door to us, clad in the drabbest of her cellar-cleaning garb, a smudge of soot on her rosy cheek.

Mrs. Handsomebody ordered sardines for tea, and had the silver tea-pot brought out. She also dressed for the occasion, adding a jet bracelet, seldom seen, to her toilet.

All went well, till, at bedtime, The Seraph could not be found. Becoming alarmed, Mrs. Handsomebody, at last, opened the door of the forbidden parlour, Angel and I peering from behind her, hoping, yet fearing, to discover the recreant.

Truly the gods had a mind to The Seraph. His was ever the cream of every adventure. There he was, lolling at ease, in a tasselled velvet chair, just beneath the portrait of Mr. Handsomebody. Lolling at ease, and smoking a gold-tipped cigarette, which, he afterwards confessed, he had got from Bill, in trade for a piece of India-rubber.

Like an old-timer he handled it, watching the smoke-wreaths above his head with the tranquil gaze of an elderly club-man.

145

"Merciful Heaven!" screamed Mrs. Handsomebody, clutching Angel and me for support. "Are you demented, Alexander? Do you realize what you are doing?"

The Seraph drew a long puff, looking straight into her eyes, before he replied: then, in a tone of gentle seriousness, he said:

"Knob-less obleedge."

Chapter IX

The Cobbler And His Wife

I

Bootlaces had become of immense importance to us, since a lack of them always meant a visit to the cobbler to buy new ones. They were comparatively easy to break, or to tie in knots that even Mary Ellen's strong fingers could not undo. Then there were tongues. One could always dislocate a tongue. At any rate, the boots of one of the three were always needing attention.

"Bless me!" our governess would exclaim, wrathfully, "Another heel off! One would think you did it purposely. And boots such a price! Just think of your poor father in South America, working day in and day out to provide you with boots, which you treat with no more consideration than if they were horseshoes—well, to the cobbler's then—and tell him to mind his charges. It should cost no more than sixpence."

The cobbler lived in the tiniest of a group of tiny houses that huddled together, in a panicky fashion, in a narrow street behind Mrs. Handsomebody's house. From an upper window we could look down on their roofs, where the plump, Cathedral pigeons used to congregate to gossip and sun themselves.

You went down three stone steps into the cobbler's shop. There he always sat at work by his bench, tapping away at the sole of a shoe, or stitching leather with his strange needle. His hands fascinated us by their coat of smooth oily dirt. Never cleaner, never dirtier, always the same useful, glove-like covering. Did he go to bed with them so? How jolly! we thought. His face, too, was of extraordinary interest. It was so thin that the sharp bones could be seen beneath the dusky skin, and he would twitch his nostrils at the breeze that came in his open window, for all the world like an eager brown hare. His hair curled so tightly over his head that one knew he could never pull a comb through it, and we were sure he was far too sensible to try.

Mrs. Handsomebody said he was half gypsy, and not to be encouraged. Mary Ellen said, God help him with that wife of his.

He bred canaries.

All about the low window their wooden cages hung. Even from the darkest corners of the shop bursts of song leaped like little flames and yellow breasts bloomed like daffodils. When the cobbler tapped a shoe with his hammer, they sang loudest, making a wild and joyous din.

Thus they were all busy together when we entered on this winter morning, carrying Angel's heelless boot, wrapped in a newspaper.

"Good-morning, Mr. Martindale," said Angel, above the din, "you see I've got another heel off, so I'm wearing my Sunday boots, and Mrs. Handsomebody says it shouldn't be above sixpence, please."

The cobbler ceased his tapping, and all the birds stopped to listen:

"Good-morning, little masters," he said, in his soft voice. "What wild things your feet are to be sure. Try as I will, I cannot tame them. You might as well try to keep three wild ponies shod." He undid the parcel and turned the boot over in his hands. "Sixpence, did she say? Nay, tell her a shilling, for the sole needs stitching as well."

"Oh, but you must keep that for another day," said Angel, "so we can come again."

"How she tries to keep you down," said the cobbler. "How old are you now?"

I replied to this. "Angel's ten, and I'm nine, and The Seraph's six."

"Just the brave age for the woods. I wish I had my old van again, and could take you on the road with me. You'd learn something of forest ways in no time. Shall you wait for this?"

Wait for it? Rather. We established ourselves about him; The Seraph climbed beside him on the bench; Angel took possession of his tools, handing them to him as required; while I busied myself in plentifully oiling a strip of leather. The birds chirped and pecked above our heads.

Angel asked: "Did you do much cobbling in the van, Mr. Martindale?"

"Ay, cobbling and tinkering too. The forest birds liked to hear me just the same as those canaries. Especially the tinkering. They'd

148

crowd about and sing fit to burst their throats—wood-thrushes, finches, and all sorts. Then, I used to stop at village fairs and take in a nice bit of silver. For my missus could play the concertina, and I had a cage of lovebirds that could tell fortunes and do tricks."

A strange voice spoke from the passage behind the shop.

"Ay. Comical tricks lovebirds do. And cruel tricks, love. I've been tricked by 'em."

"Better lie down, Ada," said Martindale. "Or make tea. That'll quiet ye." He rose and went to the door, closing it softly. But he had barely seated himself again, when there came a scream from the passage.

"Look what you've did, you villain, you've shut me in the door! Oh! oh! I'm trapped in this comical passage! Loose me quick!"

Martindale sprang to the door, where a strip of red petticoat showed that his wife was indeed caught, and went out into the passage, speaking in a soothing tone, and leading her away.

"I fink I'll go," whispered The Seraph.

"Don't be silly," I assured him, "the cobbler will take care she don't hurt us."

"She's a character, isn't she?" said Angel, borrowing a phrase from Mary Ellen.

Martindale returned then, sat down on his bench, and, smoothing his leather apron, resumed his work with composure.

"I fink," said The Seraph, "I hear Mrs. Handsomebody calling. I better be off."

"Bide a little while," said Martindale, "and I'll tell you a first rate story—about birds too. Then you'll forget your fright, little master, eh?"

The Seraph moved closer to him, and the canaries burst into a fury of song.

"It's wonderful what birds know," he began. "News flies as fast among 'em as wind on the heath, and if you do an injury to one, the

149

others'll never forgive it. For though they may fight among themselves, they'll all join together against one wicked cruel man."

The canaries ceased their singing, and fluttered against the bars.

"Just look at Coppertoes," said the cobbler, pointing to a large ruffled bird, "he's heard this tale often afore, yet it always excites him. He'll peck at his perch; and beat his wings for hours after it. Won't you, my pet?"

Coppertoes crouched on his perch, his beak open, making little hissing sounds.

"Well, there was a man," went on the cobbler, "a student fellow he was, who was always making queer messes with chemicals, and fancying he was about to discover some wonderful new combination. He lived in a top room in a high, narrow house, well on towards three hundred years ago. And all those years, a family of song-sparrows, and their descendants, had nested under the eaves directly above his window. Hatched out their young; fed them; and taught them to fly. Very well. This student fellow was all in a fever one morning because he believed that, at last, his great discovery was all but perfect. Just a few hours more and he would have it in the hollow of his hand. But he could not rightly fasten his brain to work because of the constant cheeping of the young sparrows under the eaves. Every time the mother bird brought them a moth or worm they raised a chorus of yells; and when she flew away, they cheeped for her to come back again.

"The student-fellow shut his window, but it did not keep out the noise. Then he flung open the window and waved his arms and shouted at them. But they only cheeped the louder. Now a dreadful rage took hold on him. With his heart full of murder, he fetched a basin in which he had put some poisonous drug. He set fire to this and set it on the window sill just below the nest. Then, with a triumphal smile, he shut the window fast, leaving the fledglings to perish in the fumes that rose, thick and deadly from the basin.

"For hours he worked, and, at last, to his great joy, he figured out the amazing problem that was to be a gain to the whole world. He was so tired that he clean forgot the little birds, and flung himself, face down, on his bed to rest. He did not wake until the next morning at seven. It was so dark that he had to strike a light to see the face of his watch. Now he knew that it should not be dark at either seven in the morning or seven at night; and he felt very

150

strange. The room was full of the unclean smells of his chemicals, and he groped his way to the window to get air. But the outdoor air was murky and he saw that a heavy cloud had settled just above the chimney pots. This cloud seemed to palpitate, as though made of a million beating wings. Down below he could hear the clatter of wooden clogs on the cobble stones, as people were running in a panic to the Town Hall. The big bell of it began to ring, but in a muffled way as though borne down by the cloud. The student guessed that a meeting was being called.

"He remembered the sparrows then, and he craned his neck to see the nest. There was the little mother-bird sitting in the nest with her wings outstretched to protect the nestlings from the deadly fumes. Her beak was wide open and she was quite dead."

The Seraph's breast heaved and his tears began to drop on the cobbler's leather apron. Coppertoes squatted beneath his swing, striking it angrily with his shoulders so that it swung violently. All the other birds were silent.

Steadily working at the shoe the cobbler proceeded: "The terrible truth was borne to the student then, and he knew that the cock sparrow, on finding his mate and her young ones thus foully murdered, had flown swiftly to the king of all the birds, and told him of the deed. The king had summoned great battalions of birds, from fierce eagles and owls (these last rushing from their dark hiding places) down to fluttering little wrens and tomtits. 'Twas of those that the great cloud was made, and it hung just over the town like a dark wave that would soon smother the townsfolk.

"The student caught up the paper where he had writ the great discovery and made for the street, running along with the rest of the folk, and ready to drop with fear of the great press of wings above them. When he got to the Town Hall, he found the whole town huddled together there, even new mothers with their babes, like young birds; and, in a moment the beadle had swung the great doors shut. In there they could scarce see each other's fearful faces; but the student clumb up on the council table, and he told out bravely enough how it was all his doing, and since he had brought it to pass, he was prepared to go out and face the birds alone.

"But first he handed over the paper to the Mayor, and charged him to guard it stoutly, for it was about the most precious thing on earth. Then he called—'Good-bye! friends,' and went, since there was no

151

time to spare; for the birds were beginning to hammer like hail on the windows with their beaks, especially the cranes and flamingos.

"When the door had clanged behind him the women mourned aloud, for they knew they would never see him again. A great tumult rose outside as of a hurricane, and it grew pitch dark. After a spell, the noise ceased, and the cloud lifted, and a shaft of sunlight slanted across the hall. The village tailor opened the door, for the mayor and the beadle were sore afeared. There was not a bird in sight, though the ground was inches deep in feathers they had dropped. As for the student, no one ever saw him again. Whether the birds had carried him off bodily to some secret place, or whether they had torn him piecemeal, no one knew."

The Seraph sniffled. "It's nice and twagic," he said.

"What became of his great discovery?" asked Angel.

"Ay, you may well ask that. Why, the mayor said it was bewitched and held it in the flame of a candle till there was naught left of it but cinders.... Now, here is your boot, little master, good as new, and the cost but one shilling."

II

When we entered the house, we heard voices in the parlour, and found our governess there, superintending Mary Ellen at work. Mary Ellen was carefully brushing and dusting the plumage of the stuffed birds.

I stared with a new interest at those feathered members of our household, who held themselves so coldly aloof from the rest of us; asking neither gift of chickweed nor of sugar, disdaining the very air we breathed. Who knew but that yonder sad-eyed hawk had helped to tear the student! "Piecemeal" the cobbler's word for it—one could picture him with some bloody fragment, shooting straight upward, his wide pinions spread.

Mrs. Handsomebody was speaking in a complaining way to Angel.

"A shilling! 'Tis ridiculous. For such a paltry piece of work. I shall go around that way when we take our walk and protest against such extortion. I said sixpence to you when you set out."

"I know," replied Angel, "but he said it was worth a shilling."

"You see, he has a wife to keep," put in The Seraph, "and live birds to feed."

Mary Ellen withdrew her head from the interior of the glass case.

"Oh'm," she said, very red in the face, "it's thrue that Misther Martindale needs every penny he can lay hands on, for his wife is no good to him at all, and he has to hire a charwoman to clane up for her."

"Then," said Mrs. Handsomebody, "I shall seek a shoemaker who has no such encumbrance. Is the woman feeble-minded or a sloven?"

"Faith, she's both 'm, and ivery day she's gettin' worse than she do be. I've heard her say sich things whin I've been in the shop that me very sowl-case shivered."

"What sort of things?"

"Well," said Mary Ellen, circling her duster on the glasses, so that she might still be said to be working as she talked, "the other day whin I called for me slippers wid the satin bows on—"

"I disapprove of those bows."

"—She was in the passage beyant, and just the voice of her came through the crack o' the dure. She says, says she: 'If a body was to fall—an' fall—an' fall—and there was naught to stop him, it's comical to think where he'd light on.'... Her voice was as solemn as the church organ, 'm. Another day she says: 'If I could only git the moon out of this passage, there'd be room for my head to whirl round and round!' 'Excuse me,' I says to the cobbler, 'I'll call for thim shoes later.'"

"What appearance has she?" inquired Mrs. Handsomebody.

"Noan at all. I've niver seed her. No one has ever seed her. She's more banshee than woman, I do belave."

True to her threat, Mrs. Handsomebody stopped at the cobbler's

153

that afternoon, at the outset of our accustomed promenade. The birds were in full chorus as we descended the steps into the shop.

The cobbler got to his feet, and touched his forehead respectfully. This pleased Mrs. Handsomebody.

"My good man," she said, "You have sadly overcharged me for putting a new heel on this child's boot. I said, when I sent it that it was worth sixpence—"

The cobbler opened his mouth to speak.

—"Now, don't interrupt," continued Mrs. Handsomebody. "I shall not ask you to refund the sixpence; but I have brought a prunella gaiter of my own which needs stitching, and I shall expect you to do it, without extra charge, if you wish to retain the patronage of my household."

Here was a test of manhood! Would Martindale, a full-grown male, submit to being bullied by a creature who wore a bustle, and a black silk apron? Alas, for the whiskered sex! He took his medicine; just as we, hedged in some fateful corner, gulped down our castor oil. Turning the gaiter over in his dark hands, he meekly assented. Mrs. Handsomebody, appeased by her easy victory, inquired after his wife.

"Oh, poorly as usual, thank you ma'am," he said.

"I should think that country life would be much better for her."

"She's even worse in the country."

"There was a sheet of an excellent religious paper wrapped about that gaiter. You might give it to her to read."

"Thank you, ma'am, I will, though she takes more comfort reading the dream-book than anything."

"Burn the dream-book. It is probably at the root of the trouble."

"No," replied the cobbler, slowly, "It all began when we lost our daughter."

Mrs. Handsomebody was touched. "That is sad indeed. How old was the child?"

"Just two days old, ma'am. We were camping in a forest when she

154

was born, and I had laid her in a little hammock among the birds, and some gypsies must have stolen her, for when I came back she was gone. She'd be eighteen now." He stroked his leather apron with trembling hands, at the same time giving me a curious look of appeal. So when Mrs. Handsomebody, after a few words of sympathy made a movement to go, I developed a strange pain in the leg, that made walking an impossibility. She consented that I should rest a while at the cobbler's, and then return home carrying the gaiter.

When Martindale and I were left alone, he cautiously opened the door into the passage, peered out, and then returned. He said softly:

"Little Master, I've got to get rid of Coppertoes. She's turned against him. She says he comes out of his cage of nights, and flies about the house, pecking at the food, and trying to make a nest in her hair. She says he stole a golden sovereign of hers and hid it in an old shoe. Isn't it a shame, and he such a lovely bird?"

"It's awful," I agreed. "What shall you do?"

"I know a man who will buy him, but he is out of town till tomorrow. Could I depend on you, little master, to keep him for me till then? If he is left here the misses will do him an injury."

"But Mrs. Handsomebody—" I faltered.

"Just put him in some out o' the way corner with a cloth over his cage, and a lump of sugar. He'll be quiet as can be, and 'twill soon be dark—"

III

With a delicious sense of secrecy, I stole past the Cathedral. Pressed against my breast was the cage that held Coppertoes. He sat quietly on his perch, very long, and slender, and bright-eyed with amazement at this sudden excursion into a new world. I wondered what he thought of the towering Cathedral, shrouded in a film of hoar frost that lent its ancient stones a bloom as delicate as the petals of flowers.

Three pigeons hopped daintily down the shallow stone steps,

155

cocking their heads inquisitively at the bird in the cage. I shouted at them, and they rose slowly to the tower above.

Silent indeed was the hall when I entered. Only the clock ticked ponderously. The house was cold, and Coppertoes seemed suddenly very fragile. How lonely he would be! I stared at the closed door of the parlour, thinking what a shame that the stuffed birds in there were not alive, so they might be company for him. Still—he was very young—and had not seen much of the world. Might he not be made to believe that they were a foreign breed that never chirped or left their perches? Anything was better than the dark and loneliness. And if he chose to sing I was sure he could not be heard through that heavy door.

Like a ghost I went in and shut the door behind me.

I held his wicker cage against the glass case. "Coppertoes," I whispered, "Other birds! Aren't they pretty? Want to get in an' play with them, old chap? See the pretty oriole? An' the owl, Coppertoes. Lovebirds, too. Want to get in, little fellow? Such a bully big cage you never saw."

I opened the door of the glass case, and cautiously introduced the bird cage. I opened the door of the cage. Coppertoes paid no heed but busied himself in pecking sharply at his lump of sugar. I urged him with my finger but still he refused to see the door. Then I took away his sugar, and poked him. With a light and careless hop he was on the threshold. He cocked his head. He spied the oriole.

An instant later he was at its throat. Feathers flew. He was back again on the roof of his cage spitting feathers out of his mouth. More feathers sailed slowly through the heavy air. Then he spied the lovebirds. With passionate fury he attacked them both at once, tearing their plumage impartially; his eye already selecting the next victim.

Though my heart thumped with apprehension, my mouth was stretched in a broad grin. I felt that I should never tire of the spectacle before me. I realized that I had always hated the stuffed birds.

Coppertoes was busy with the owl, when a piercing scream came from behind me. I turned and found Mrs. Handsomebody gazing with horrified fascination at the orgy under glass. She took three steps forward, her eyes starting with horror.

"Come to life—" she gasped, in a strangled voice—"after all these years—and gone stark mad."

She fell, at full length, across the green and red medallions of the carpet.

Then, with a rush, Mary Ellen and the charwoman, Mrs. Coe, were upon us, and, after them, my brothers.

"Lord preserve us!" cried Mary Ellen, bending above her prostrate mistress, "what has come over the poor lady to be took like this?"

"Is she dead, do you fink?" asked The Seraph, on a hopeful note.

"Well, if she is, faith! 'tis yersilves has kilt her."

"She's just in a swoond," asserted Mrs. Coe, calmly. "Wot she needs is brandy. Yus, and terbaccer smoke blowed dahn 'er froat." Mrs. Handsomebody moaned.

"Better get her out of here," suggested Angel, his eye on Coppertoes who, sated by bloodshed, lay with wings outstretched, panting on the floor of the case.

"Thrue," agreed Mary Ellen. "And shut the dure afther ye, and make yersilves scarce till tea-time, like good childer, do."

Mrs. Handsomebody was borne away by Mary Ellen and Mrs. Coe, the latter still muttering—"terbaccer smoke dahn 'er froat."

We restored Coppertoes to his wicker cage, and wrapping it in an antimacassar, hid it beneath the piano.

IV

We three sat, "making ourselves scarce," on the topmost of the steps before the front door. It was only four by the Cathedral clock, which solemnly struck the hour, but it was almost dark. It was cold and we pressed closely together for warmth. The Seraph murmured a little song of which I caught the words:

> *"The birds! The birds!*
> *He knocked the stuffing*

157

We watched the slow progress of the lamplighter along the street. Like a god, he marched solemnly, leaving new stars in his wake.

As he raised his wand and touched the lamp before our house, a new figure appeared beneath its rays, hurrying darkly towards us. It entered the gate and came in a stealthy way to where we sat. We recognized the cobbler.

"Little masters," he whispered. "She's flitted."

"Good widdance," said The Seraph, briskly. "She was too comical to be a nice wife."

"Ah, no," replied the cobbler. "She's weak in her head and bound to come to something hurtful. I'll not seek my bed this night until I've found her. I thought mayhap you'd ha' seen her pass!"

"No," replied Angel. "We didn't. But perhaps the lamplighter did."

With one accord, we hurried after the retreating figure. Hearing our footsteps, he turned and faced us beneath a newly lit lamp. Its serene radiance fell on his solemn blue-eyed face, surrounded by red whiskers.

"What's the turmoil?" he asked. "Did I forget a lamp?"

"Have ye seen a strange-appearing woman?" asked Martindale. "With a shawl about her, and mayhap remarking something about the moon, or a evil-minded canary."

The lamplighter ran his fingers through his red beard. "She warn't saying naught about canaries," he affirmed, "but she did say as how if she could once get the moon in Wumble Pool, she'd drown it."

"Wumble Pool. That's where she's gone then. I can't seem to place it."

"It's less nor a mile from here, and since my last lamp is lit, I'll not mind guiding you so far. Who be she, this woman?"

"My wife. She's fey, and I'm fearing she'll drown herself."

"It's a very bad fing to be drowned," put in The Seraph, as we all set off together. "'Cos a bath in a tub is wet enough."

158

What a chill, dark night it was growing! The Cathedral clock struck a hollow warning note as we passed. We heard the beat of wings as the pigeons settled for the night.

The Seraph grasped a hand each of the cobbler and the lamplighter, taking long manful strides to keep up with them. We seemed, indeed, a sinister company setting out on dark adventure.

Hurriedly we traversed narrow, winding streets, where night had already fallen in the shadow of clammy walls. Strange and eerie was the path between wet trees, when we had left the town behind. The lamplighter with his tall wand alight seemed like some unearthly messenger come to conduct us to goblin realms.

We spoke never a word till an open common lay before us; then the lamplighter pointing with his wand to a glimmering surface fringed by rank grass, said:

"Yon's Wumble Pool."

Wumble Pool! The very name struck a chill to our hearts.

"Yes, and there's the moon," whispered the cobbler.

It was true that the distorted image of the moon floated dimly in the Pool, as though it had indeed been caught by the mad-woman, and drowned.

"How soft the ground is!" breathed Angel.

"Ay, and the Pool has no bottom," said the lamplighter.

"I can't think she'd have the heart to do it," said Martindale.

The Seraph screamed.

"There she is! I see her! Standing in the Pool!"

We ran to the brink. A cold air struck our faces. Our feet sank ankle-deep in the mud. The cobbler did not stop, but ran on into the Pool, where the shawled figure of a woman stood, covered to the waist by the sullen, black water.

"Ada! Ada!" cried the cobbler, throwing his arms about her.

"Leave me go!" shrieked the woman. "I'm a-goin' to drownd myself!"

The struggle in the water, shattered the reflection of the moon like pale amber glass. Once they both sank into the water; the lamplighter waving his wand, and shouting. Then, at last, the four of us bent over them as they lay, huddled, on the grass at the brink.

"You'd ought to be ashamed of yourself to worrit your 'usband so," said the lamplighter, sternly.

"'Usband!" cried the woman, shrilly. "I've got no 'usband!"

The cobbler gave a cry of fear. He pulled the shawl from her head and felt the face and hair.

"God's truth!" he muttered, "I've saved the wrong woman."

"Better fwow her back again," suggested The Seraph.

"Nay, nay, little man," said the lamplighter, holding his light close to her face. "That would never do. Besides, her be young and winsome."

"I'd keep her," said Angel.

"Whoever are you, lass?" asked Martindale, in a trembling voice, "and why did you plan to make way with yourself?"

The moon shone wanly on the girl's face and wet hair.

"I'm nobody," she wailed, "and I be tired of life."

"Did you see aught of a strange woman?" asked Martindale. "One who was talking about the moon, and her head a-whirling?"

"She came right down the road ahead of me," she answered, in a weak voice, "and ran straight into the pool. When she was in, she grabbed the floating image of the moon, and she said: 'I've got you, at last, you comical villain!' And she laughed, and seemed to struggle with it, and she went down."

"That'd be her, all right," said the lamplighter.

"Ada mine, Ada mine," mourned Martindale.

Angel and The Seraph and I clutched hands, and looked shudderingly into Wumble Pool.

"That seemed to scare me like," went on the girl, "and I couldn't

160

jump right in, but I just crept, a step at a time, fearing I'd step on the body."

"No danger," said The Seraph complacently, "there's no bottom."

"One thing is certain," pronounced the lamplighter, "this young 'ooman should have some hot spirits in her inside, and be wrapped in a warm blanket, afore she's starved with the cold."

First we walked all around Wumble Pool, and poked it with sticks, but there was no sign of the cobbler's wife. Then, slowly, we retraced our steps to the town, the two men supporting the dripping girl.

A lamp burned with a ruddy glow in the room behind the shop, where all the birds were sleeping. Martindale put his charge in a chair by the hearth, and made gin-and-beer hot for everybody. The Seraph kissed the girl, and she said that she was glad after all that she was safe out of Wumble Pool.

"What is your name, my dear?" questioned Martindale.

"I don't know my name rightly, sir, for I was stole by gipsies when I was but two days old."

The cobbler gave a cry and set down his glass. "Gipsies—two days' old—" he stammered. Then he pushed back the thick hair, about her ear. "Yes, yes!" pointing to a tiny slit in the lobe, "there is the very place,—where one of my jealous birds pecked her the day she was born!" He caught her in his arms and held her, mystified but happy—.

The reunion was interrupted by a pounding at the door. It was a furious Mary Ellen, her night out completely spoiled by the search for us.

Thus we were haled before Mrs. Handsomebody, questioned, upbraided, and given, at last, a bowl of hot gruel apiece.

"You deserve," she said bitterly, "to go empty to bed, but my conscience forbids that I relax my vigilance over your health. Tomorrow, we shall see what can be done in the way of discipline."

We sat on three high-backed haircloth chairs. The steaming gruel slipped thickly into our stomachs. The hot gin had gone to our heads. Mrs. Handsomebody's head looked abnormally large to me, and seemed to be whirling round and round. Surely she was not

161

getting like the cobbler's wife! Mrs. Handsomebody was still scolding:

"You began the day by introducing a canary of the lowest proclivities into my case of stuffed birds, where he perpetrated irreparable damage—"

The Seraph interrupted, "Don't you yike live birds, Mrs. Handsomebody?"

"I prefer stuffed birds to live ones, I confess."

The Seraph said apologetically: "And I pwefer gin to gwuel—any day."

"Gin! Where did you taste gin?"

Without reply The Seraph hurried on, while Angel and I scraped our bowls:

"There was once a student fellow and he didn't yike live birds, either. He poisoned one and it died. Then he undertook a walk (this was a favourite expression of Mrs. Handsomebody's) and all the other birds pounced on him and tore him piecemeal."

Mrs. Handsomebody, with a ferocious gleam in her eye, leaned forward to catch the rest. The Seraph's voice was low and insinuating.

"I was finking"—with a chuckle—"that you might poison one of the nicest of the stuffed birds. Then you might get in the glass case wiv the others. We could lock the door on the outside and watch through the glass."

"And I expect you think they would tear me piecemeal? Is that the idea?"

"Oh, I don't know," chuckled The Seraph. "But suppose you twy it."

Chapter X

The New Day

I

I think we must have felt that he was coming, for we awoke at dawn that morning. I could barely see the silvery bars between the slats of the shutters. The Seraph was stirring in his sleep, and in a moment he whispered: "I say, John, what's that long black thing behind the door?"

"Just some clothes hung up," I whispered back.

"I fought they moved," he said. "Do you fink the wardrobe door moved, John?"

"Everything seems a little queer this morning," I replied. "I heard a whispering sort of noise at the shutters a bit ago."

Angel began to talk in his sleep.

"If three suns were to rise at six," he muttered, "how many stars would it take to make a moon?"

The Seraph began to laugh delightedly. He kicked his legs and showed all his little white teeth. Angel opened his eyes and stared at us crossly. "What a beastly row," he said. "I want to sleep some more."

The silver bars between the slats of the shutters took a golden tinge. Clearly it was to be a fine day, after a week of rain and sleet.

The chimes of the Cathedral sounded. The notes came with penetrating sweetness as though the air were cold and clear. We heard the door of Mary Ellen's room open; she descended the back stairs noisily.

The Seraph turned a somersault in the middle of the bed.

"Cwistmas is coming," he said, trying to stand on his head, "and I want a pony."

163

We threw ourselves into a general scuffle, and the old-four-poster creaked and the bolster fell to the floor.

Then up the cavernous backstairs came the peal of the front door bell. We heard Mary Ellen drop the poker and run through the house. It was an unheard of hour for the front door bell to ring. We sat up in bed in stiffened attitudes of expectancy. Mary Ellen was mounting the front stair. She rapped loudly at Mrs. Handsomebody's bedroom door. There were whispers. Then Mrs. Handsomebody's voice came decidedly:

"Go about your work with the utmost speed. Say nothing to the boys of this. I shall tell them when they have had their breakfast."

In a moment she appeared at our door in her purple dressing-gown, an expression of repressed excitement on her face. A sunbeam slanting through the passage rested on the fringe of curl-papers about her head so that she looked like some elderly saint wearing a rather ragged halo.

"I have received news," she announced, with more than usual firmness, "which will make it necessary for us to rise immediately. Dress as quickly as you can, and help your little brother. What a state you have got that bed into! You deserve to be punished." She stood for a moment, her eyes resting on us with a curious look, then, with a sigh, she turned away and went back to her room.

At breakfast she still wore her dressing-gown, an unprecedented laxity. Beside her on the table-cloth lay a crumpled piece of buff paper. So it was by telegram that the news had come. Instantly I thought. The telegram is from father. He is coming home. Maybe he is on his way. In London even! The food would not go down my throat. Shudders of excitement shook me.

I looked at Angel. Taking advantage of Mrs. Handsomebody's absorption he was spreading a second spoonful of sugar over his porridge. The Seraph was staring, spoon in hand, into Mrs. Handsomebody's set face. He said—

"Mrs. Handsomebody, if I was to smile at you, would you smile back at me?"

"Alexander," replied Mrs. Handsomebody, "I hope I have never been found wanting in courtesy. But, at present, I should prefer to see you eat your breakfast with as much speed as possible. John, eat your porridge."

"I can't, please."

"Eat it instantly, sir."

"I can't," I repeated, beginning to blubber, "I want to see father!"

"Eat your porridge and you shall see him. He will be here at ten o'clock. Silence, now, no uproar. My nerves are under quite enough strain." She poured herself fresh tea, and continued:

"There will be no tasks today. After breakfast you will put on your best jackets and collars, and sit in the parlour until he arrives. I implore you to be as composed as possible."

The questions that poured from us were hushed by a gesture of her inflexible, white hand. Dazed by the news, we were herded back to our bedroom, hurried into stiff white collars and hustled into shining Sunday shoes. There was the sound of cold water tinkling in the basin; of straining bootlaces; and of the creaking of a loose board in the floor every time Mary Ellen stepped on it. Scarcely a word was spoken. Now that what we had so long strained towards was at hand we stood breathless before the immensity of it. The long year and nine months at Mrs. Handsomebody's fell like a heavy curtain between us and the past. Our father's face had grown hazy to us. I think The Seraph only pretended to remember. His coming had been held over our heads so long, as a time of swift retribution, that a feeling of doubt, almost terror, mingled with our joy.

At last we were ready. With shining faces, burning ears, and quickly tapping hearts, we went soberly down the stairs. The door of the parlour stood wide open. Mrs. Handsomebody, herself, was dusting the case of stuffed birds, whose plumage, sadly thinned by the attentions of Coppertoes, seemed to quiver with expectancy.

We were instructed to wait inside the iron gate, at the front, until train time, when we were to be recalled to the parlour, and take our places on three chairs, already ranged in a row for us. Thus we were to be displayed by Mrs. Handsomebody, to our sire.

We found Granfa polishing the brass on the front door, his white locks bobbing as he rubbed.

"Oh, Granfa," we cried, "have you heard the news?"

"Ess fay," he replied, straightening his back, "for thiccy Mary Ellen came a-galloping at top speed to ask me to shine the brasses for 'ee, knowing I have a wonderful art that way. The poor Zany was all in a mizmaze."

"Are you glad father's coming?"

"Glad! I be so joyful as a bulfinch in springtime. See how the very face of Natur' be lit up for the grand occasion."

The sky had, indeed, become deeply blue, and a great pink cloud hung above the Cathedral like a welcoming banner. There had been frost in the night forming thin ice over the puddles in the road. All those reflected the serene pink of the cloud, a blue pigeon picked his way delicately among them. A sweet-smelling wind swayed the moist brown limbs of the elm trees. All the world seemed like a great organ attuned to joy.

"Suppose," suggested Angel, "that we just race around to the cobbler's and tell him the news. The Dragon is too busy to miss us."

The very thing! It would take only a few minutes and would be something to do to pass the time. Softly we slipped through the iron gate; lightly we hastened along the shining wet street; under the shadow of the Cathedral, whose spire seemed to taper to the sky; down narrow, winding Henwood Street till we reached the cobbler's shop.

Martindale was standing in the open door his face raised as though he were drinking in the fragrance of the morning. A chorus of bird song came from inside.

"Hallo, Mr. Martindale," Angel shouted.

"What do you suppose? Father's coming home."

"He'll be here In less than two hours," I panted.

The cobbler put a dark hand on a shoulder of each. "That's grand news, little masters," he said. "But I hope he won't take you so far away that I shall never see you. The birds like you too. They never sing so loud as when you are in the shop."

While he was speaking we heard footsteps coming quickly down Henwood street around the corner. They were quick, sharp footsteps that rang on the frosty air. "It's curious," said the cobbler, "how footsteps sound here. I think it's the Cathedral walls that give that ringing sound."

166

We turned to watch for the approaching pedestrian. We wondered who he was that walked with such an eager, springing step. He turned the corner. He faced us. Then he laughed out loud and said, "Hello!"

We were, for a second, simply staggered. We made incoherent noises like young animals. Then we were snatched by rough tweed arms, a small, stiff moustache rasped our cheeks, and—"Father!" we squealed, at last, in chorus.

"I found I could catch an early train," he said, "so I just hopped on, for I was in a desperate hurry to see you. What are you doing here, at this hour?" He stared at the cobbler.

"This is Mr. Martindale," I explained. "He mends our boots, and tells us stories, and he's got a bird named Coppertoes."

"So you are a friend of my boys," said father. "Ay. And they're grand little lads, sir. I have a daughter of my own I'm very proud of, sir. She was lost for seventeen years, and your sons helped me to find her."

His daughter came to the door then to call him to breakfast. She had a yellow braid over each shoulder, and Coppertoes was sitting on her wrist with a piece of chickweed in his bill. Father stopped to admire them both.

"By George," he said, when we had left them, "if all your friends are as interesting as those, I should like to meet them."

"They are that," I said, happily, "and here's another of them."

It was Granfa, standing at the gate, his blue eyes staring with amazement. He raised his broom to his shoulder and stood at attention as we drew near.

"What a sight for the nation!" he exclaimed. "Welcome home my dear son-in-law. I be terrible proud to hand my charges over to 'ee. Us have got along famous while you was over to South Ameriky."

I trembled for fear father should say something to hurt Granfa's feelings, but he seemed to understand him at once, and shook him by the hand, and made him a present of some tobacco on the spot.

II

"Merciful Heaven!" screamed Mrs. Handsomebody. "Davy!" "Mr. Curzon!" She clutched her curl-papers in one hand and the front of her purple wrapper in the other. "We did not expect you for an hour yet."

Father laughed. "Well, I've saved you some of the trouble of preparing by coming early. How very well you are looking. And how well-cared-for the children. I'm delighted. I think I shall take them over to the hotel where my luggage has been sent and have a talk with them and come back later. Will that suit you?"

But Mrs. Handsomebody insisted that he have a proper breakfast, and installed us in the parlour while she retired to assume the decent armour of the day.

Father sat facing the stuffed birds. He put The Seraph on his knee, and Angel and I hung on either side of him. We were suddenly shy of him, and it seemed enough to be near him, and to feel the all-surrounding power and protection of him. His cheeks were incredibly sun-browned, with a ruddy glow beneath; his moustache and the hair at his temples were almost golden. I liked the greenish grey of his tweed suit that seemed to match his clear, wide-open eyes.

He made a wry face at the stuffed birds and then he whispered: "Old chaps, have you been happy here?"

We nodded. The past was gone. What did it matter! "Oh, but, we want to be wiv you! Don't leave us," breathed The Seraph, burrowing his face into the rough tweed shoulder.

Angel and I burrowed against him too. "Don't leave us again," we whispered.

He began to kiss us, and to rumple our heads, and to bite The Seraph's cheek. The Seraph, drunk with joy, jumped down, and pulling open the door of the glass case tried to drag a lovebird from its perch to present to father. We were just able to stop him when our governess returned.

She was dignified and smiling, in black satin and a gold chain. Mary Ellen had the breakfast laid in the dining-room and we sat about him, watching him eat. With what admiration we beheld his

168

masterful attack on the bacon and eggs! It became awe when we saw the quantity of marmalade that he spread upon his toast.

And Mrs. Handsomebody beamed fatuously at him!

Between mouthfuls he talked. "Do you remember how I used to call you Wiggie? And the time I hid the white rat in your bonnet box?"

Mrs. Handsomebody cackled. The Seraph kicked the table leg, unreproved. I drifted after Mary Ellen to the kitchen. "Isn't he fine?" I bragged.

"Divil a finer," agreed she.

"And 'tis yersilf, Masther John," she added, "is the very spit av him. Shure it's you should be the proud bye."

"And, Mary Ellen, you are to come and live with us, you know, and have all the 'followers' you want."

"Och," she laughed, "I'm done wid followers, me dear. To tell ye the truth, Mr. Watlin and I are plannin' to git hitched up, before the New Year. An uncle of his have died and left him enough to start him in the butcherin' business on his own account. So maybe you'll dance at me weddin' yet."

"I'll give you a nice present, Mary Ellen, dear," I promised, putting my arm around her.

"Yes," she went on, squeezing me, "and the cook next door was tellin' me last night, that the word is goin' about that Miss Margery an' Misther Harry is engaged too. So there's love in the air, Masther John. D'ye mind the time 'twas yersilf was in love wid little Miss Jane? Bless yer little heart."

I fled back to the dining-room.

Mary Ellen was now dispatched to blow her whistle for a hansom, and almost before we realized it we found ourselves rolling smoothly to the hotel where father was to stay.

Next, we were in his very room, exploring, with adventurous fingers, all his admirable, tobacco-smelling belongings. When his back was turned, Angel even unsheathed his razor and flourished it, for one hair-lifting second. But father caught him and promised that he should become acquainted with the razor-strop also, if he grew too bold.

We went out and bought chocolates and toys and brought them back to his room to play with. The morning passed in a delicious dream. Then luncheon downstairs with him, the eyes of many people on us.

Among them I discovered, before long, the laughing blue eyes of Lady Simon. She was not looking at me, but very eagerly at father, as though she were trying to make him see her. In a moment she succeeded, and, without a word of explanation to us he jumped up and strode across to the table where she and Lord Simon sat. The Seraph ran after him and was gathered into her arms while she smiled and talked to father over his curls.

"Wonder if she's askin' him for another lapis lazarus necklace," said Angel, his mouth full of charlotte russe, "she'd better not, 'cos we're all he can afford now."

I did not like the idea either, so when father came back with The Seraph hanging to his coat tails, I remarked, with some asperity:

"She said you nearly ruined yourself once to buy her a pair of cream-coloured ponies."

"Yes, and a lapis lazarus necklace," added Angel, accusingly.

"I want a cweam-culled pony!" shouted The Seraph.

Father leaned over us with almost the expression of Mrs. Handsomebody in his eye.

"You shall all have ponies," he said, "any old colour you like, cream, or pink, or blue, if you'll shut up and be good."

Dazzled by the vision of a herd of rainbow-coloured ponies we suffered ourselves to be led in silence from the dining-room. Outside, father said, still with the look of Mrs. Handsomebody in his eye:

"I have to make a call on a lady in Argyle Road, my godmother. Do you feel prepared to come, and be good boys, or shall I send you back to your governess?"

"Argyle Road!" exclaimed Angel. "That's where Giftie lived."

"Want to see Giftie!" came from The Seraph, "and Colin."

"Are you going to be good?"

"Rather," said Angel. "Please take us."

Another hansom was called. We were quite prepared to see it stop before the large square house where Giftie lived. It stopped. There was a clamour of barks from three Scottish terriers as we entered the gate. In a second I had Giftie in my arms; her little, hard wriggling body pressed to my breast; her little red tongue showing between her pointed white teeth. She was wild with the joy of welcoming us, but Colin walked solemnly away, his tail very much in the air. The third dog I felt sure was one of Giftie's pups. "His name is Tam," shouted the tall grey-haired lady, having suddenly appeared, and I discovered then that we were in the drawing-room, and pulled off my cap, and smiled up at her.

"I've been saving him for you," she went on, "hoping you would turn up. The other two are sold. But Tam is for you boys, and oh, Davy," turning to father, "you must let me have them for Christmas. We shall have an enormous Christmas Tree, and look! it's beginning to snow."

It was true. Great white flakes were softly whirling past the windows, shutting us away from the outer world. The fire seemed to burn the brighter for them, the air seemed full of happiness and gay adventure. We bent over our new possession on the hearthrug in ecstasy. Tam, in ferocious playfulness, tried to show us all part of his body at once. But when we overcame him, and pinned him down, he lay limply, with his tongue out at one side, and the promise of many a future romp in his roguish brown eyes. Giftie brought a woollen bedroom slipper from upstairs to worry for our amusement. Even Colin grew friendly. The talk went on above our heads, the far-off talk of grown-ups. But stay—it was not so incomprehensible after all! What was it she was saying? A pantomime! A deserving Charity. Had tickets. Suppose we take the children. Would it bore Davy? Davy said it wouldn't.

Was all our new life to be a whirl like this? Now we were back in the hansom cab bowling through the madly dancing snowflakes. Now we were back at Mrs. Handsomebody's having tea with a double portion of jam; being scrubbed and brushed, and warned of our behaviour, sliding on the slippery soles of new boots; sniffing the fresh linen of clean handkerchiefs; watching Mrs. Handsomebody tie her bonnet strings with trembling fingers.

171

In a four-wheeler now, squeezed very closely together; the wheels moving heavily through the ever-deepening snow; lights flashing by the snowy windows, father's leg and boot pressing against me cruelly but giving a delicious sense of protection and good fellowship. Then the blazing light, and heat, and pressing crowd of the lobby; a sense of terror lest the pompous man who took tickets would refuse to accept those tendered by father; immense relief, as a thin, bounding individual led us down the sloping aisle. Father's guiding hand on our shoulders; we were in our seats.

On my right sat father, and beyond him Angel. On my left The Seraph and Mrs. Handsomebody, her hands clasped tensely in her lap. But who was that in the golden light beyond Angel? Who indeed but our old friend Captain Pegg who had come, it appeared, with Giftie's mistress. Lucky Angel to be next him, laughing and whispering with him! Then, lucky me to be pushed between the seats to shake his hand.

"Shiver my timbers, John," he whispered, "but I have great days to tell you of! Days of plunder and bloodshed, my hearty. I went back to the old life, for a while, you know. Look here!" He drew aside his coat and around his waist I saw that he wore a belt of alligator skin into which was thrust a curved and glittering bowie knife!

The curtain was going up. I was pulled back into my seat. My pulses throbbed as scene by scene the pantomime was disclosed before my happy eyes. Here was I, John Curzon, part of quite as good a play as yon. Pirates, love, fluttering banners, swashbuckling clowns, life stretched before me, a jolly adventure with Angel and The Seraph always there to share the fun. Now the Seraph's head had dropped to Mrs. Handsomebody's lap. He was half asleep. Her black kid hand patted his back. She was gazing with a rapt smile at the stage.

The pantomime was nearly over. The night of danger and dark alarm was past. Rosy morning broke upon the mountain side, and Columbine, reclining in a pearl-pink shell, opened her eyes and smiled upon a flowery world.

I felt father's cheek against my head. His hand covered mine. He whispered:

"Happy, John?"

I nodded, clutching his fingers. And so we met the New Day together.